ALSO BY KAY SALTER

Twelfth Summer

Thirteenth Summer

Fourteenth Summer

Fifteenth Summer

To order copies, please contact: jsalter8@hotmail.com

Sixteenth Summer

The Sarah Bowers Series

Kay Salter

authorHOUSE®

AuthorHouse™
1663 Liberty Drive
Bloomington, IN 47403
www.authorhouse.com
Phone: 1-800-839-8640

First published by AuthorHouse   09/21/2011

ISBN: 978-1-4670-3484-5 (sc)
ISBN: 978-1-4670-3483-8 (hc)
ISBN: 978-1-4670-3482-1 (ebk)

Library of Congress Control Number: 2011916288

Printed in the United States of America

Any people depicted in stock imagery provided by Thinkstock are models, and such images are being used for illustrative purposes only.
Certain stock imagery © Thinkstock.

This book is printed on acid-free paper.

Kind Words

"Kay's 'Summer' books make me feel like I grew up in Beaufort, or wish I had."   **Terry Linder**

"The books make me cry and sing at the same time."   **Nancy G. Willis**

"I anxiously await each new book. You will enjoy and be blessed by her books."   **Mary Jo Pearce**

"I can't put Ms. Kay's books down. I truly enjoy them and I am waiting for book five.   **Tammy G. Lewis**

"The Sarah Bowers books are like an addiction—you just can't get enough."   **Lisa Paul**

"Once you start reading you can't put them down."   **Becky Saunders**

In Appreciation

To DeeDot who made all things possible.

Gratitudes

A very special thanks to Faye and Jim Brown for the use of their 'fish house' as the cover for 'Sixteenth Summer.' Capt. Jake's dock and fish house from the 1940's disappeared years ago on the wings of a passing hurricane.

I am grateful to Samantha Goodwin for taking time from her busy college schedule to pose as Sarah Bowers for the cover of 'Sixteenth Summer.'

Capt. Jake sat on his dock and dispensed shards of wisdom to all who would listen. Jimmy Piner, much like Capt. Jake, has a wealth of knowledge and 'salty' stories for all who are fortunate enough to hear them. No makeup had to be used for the cover picture. Jimmy Piner really is that old.

Always, I am grateful to Mary Beth, Dot and Amy for tirelessly cleaning and correcting each book before publication.

Contents

Chapter 1

"I don't care what anybody says! I'm taking the bus to Beaufort!" Joshua Bowers brought his fist down firmly on the sturdy oak table in the kitchen of his Raleigh home. The old table had been his grandparents' since his father was a child. Now, another generation was sitting around it making plans for the summer.

James Bowers stared at his son. "You'd better have a good explanation for your behavior. Such a display of temper is not allowed at this table."

"Daddy," said Joshua, pleading. "I'm only ten years old, and too young to die." Joshua, always dramatic, looked around the table, searching for a sympathetic face.

"Explain," his father snapped, patience growing thin.

Joshua looked over at his older sister, Sarah. She was sitting, elbows on the table, chin resting on her hands.

"I heard Mama promise Sarah she could do the driving!"

Sarah sat up and glared at her brother. "What's wrong with that?" she demanded. "I've had a driver's license for three months, and not one single wreck."

"That's only because people see you coming and get out of the way!"

1

"Mama!"

Peggy Bowers rolled her eyes and shook her head, causing short, blonde curls to bounce and shiver. "Joshua, you're too young to ride the bus by yourself. Besides, it would take all day. Beaufort is over one hundred and fifty miles away with stops in every town . . ."

" . . . and every mail box," added James. "Joshua can stay in Raleigh with me this summer. I welcome his company. It gets pretty lonesome rattling around in this house by myself for weeks and weeks." James grinned at his son, "Besides, Bowers Chemical Co. could use someone who knows how to operate a push broom. On Saturdays we can clean house, wash clothes and buy groceries. On Sunday we'll go to Sunday school and church and have dinner with Grandma and Grandpa Bowers." James paused, and then added, "You can have the rest of Sunday afternoon off to rest for work on Monday."

Joshua thought fast. "I can't break Papa Tom and Granny Jewel's heart."

Quickly Sarah answered. "We'll all manage somehow without you, little brother. When we're swimming, fishing and eating Clara's good cooking, we'll always think of you. Oh, and let's not forget the breeze off the ocean that keeps us cool on hot days. You think of us when the top pops off the thermometer up here in Raleigh."

Amy, the younger daughter, and baby of the family, spoke. "I wanna see Papa Tom and Granny Jool. Take me with you, Sarah."

"Thank you, Amy. I promise to drive carefully and deliver you safely to our grandparents."

Peggy Bowers got up to stir a pot of spaghetti sauce that had been bubbling slowly during the discussion. The room grew silent as each inhaled the spicy Italian odor that was rapidly filling the kitchen. Sarah filled a pot with water for noodles and set it on the stove to boil. She turned around and said, "We can take Frisky to the coast with us. He loves to go swimming as chase shore birds."

"Frisky is my dog. Papa Tom and I found him."

"If I remember correctly, Frisky found you," said the father.

"Oh, all right." The boy heaved a deep sigh. "Frisky and I will go with you, but I'm only doing it for him."

"Your are a wonderful person, Joshua, truly wonderful to make such a sacrifice for your loyal pet," said his big sister, her remarks tinged with sarcasm.

There was little time the following week for more discussion on transportation. School closed and friends said goodbye for the summer. In every bedroom an open suitcase rapidly filled with Sunday clothes, summer outfits and favorite toys.

James Bowers embraced each member of his family early one June morning and walked to the car with last minute instructions. "I expect the three of you to mind your mother and grandparents. If I hear of any bickering or arguing, you'll come back to Raleigh with me after the Fourth of July weekend."

"Yes sir," the three chorused. Sarah, in the driver's seat sighed, "Mama, why does he always include me, as if I were a little child?" Peggy Bowers looked at her sixteen year old daughter. She certainly didn't resemble a child. With long dark brown hair, gray eyes and full red lips, her first born looked more like a grown woman.

"Perhaps it's because you and Joshua often act the same age." Their mother changed the subject. "Do you want me to drive until we're out of the city?"

"Yes, Mama," came a voice from the back seat. "It will give Frisky and me a chance to get our crash helmets on."

Sarah turned around and attempted to swat her brother on the leg. He was anticipating her move, and slid out of reach.

The tall buildings soon gave way to gracious homes along tree lined avenues. After leaving the city, they passed fields of tall, green corn stalks and tobacco with wide, green leaves. Air rushing through the open windows felt cooler after the heat of the city.

"Watch the speed limit, Sarah. You don't want to get a ticket for going too fast."

"It's all right, Mama," said Sarah smiling at her mother. "I'll tell the patrolman I'm anxious to see my grandparents. I'm sure he'll understand."

"Don't be too sure," said Peggy, frowning. "His job is to see that we get there in one piece."

Sarah, both hands on the wheel, realized her life and the lives of her loved ones were her responsibility.

"I promise to be careful, Mama," Sarah answered.

"Tires are more reliable now," said the mother. "During the war, you couldn't buy tires for love nor money unless you had ration tickets. After the war, the rubber was so thin, you could almost see through it."

Sarah slowed to the speed limit as they drove through each small town. There were at least two traffic lights on every main street. In downtown Goldsboro they had to wait for a traffic light to change. Mother and daughter looked in a dress shop window. Seeing a cute outfit, Sarah exclaimed, "Mama, maybe we need to park and go shopping. After all, this year we can wear the same size."

"It's too hot," said Joshua. "You'll be in there all day, and Amy and I will cook."

"He's right, Sarah. We could take the kids in with us, but the animals would suffer." In the back seat with the two younger children were Frisky the dog, and Spooky, the white cat Sarah had rescued from under the Methodist church in Beaufort.

"I'm dying of thirst, Mama," said Joshua, hoping the threat of a shopping trip had passed.

"OK, Son, we'll stop at a filling station outside of town, get a cold drink and use the bathroom."

"Pooky woke up and wants to potty," announced Amy. The cat, content to nap most of the trip, grew restless. "Raise the window before he decides to jump out," instructed their mother.

"Frisky wants to get out and stretch his legs," said Joshua, using an expression he had heard before.

"If you let him out you better hold him tight," said Sarah. "If he gets away, he'll stretch his legs all right, half way across the county."

After several miles had passed, Sarah started to pull into a filling station.

"No, no, let's not stop here. There are too many men standing around. It makes me feel uncomfortable," said Peggy.

Finally, they saw a station with no one visible, that appeared clean. "Please, Mama, I'm dying back here," announced Joshua.

Sarah pulled in and parked in front of the gasoline pump. An attendant came out to wash the windshield. "Fill 'er up, Ma'am?" he asked Peggy, his eyes on Sarah.

"Yes, please, and check the oil and water." She turned to her children. "We don't want to stay long. Your grandparents are probably sitting on the porch watching every car that goes by."

Peggy found a large, red cooler near the cash register. Lifting the lid, she plunged her hand into the ice and retrieved four bottles of Coca-Cola. They stood and enjoyed their drinks, putting the empty bottles in a wooden crate near by.

"I'm going to let Frisky stretch his legs, Mama," said Joshua, letting the screen door of the station slam behind him.

"I dread getting back in that hot car," said Peggy. "It's actually cool in here with that big fan overhead."

"Just think how cool it will be when we get to Beaufort. I can feel that breeze already," answered Sarah. The three stepped out in time to see Joshua open the car door. Before he could grab Frisky's leash, Spooky darted from the open door. Behind him, barking every breath was Frisky, his blue leash bouncing merrily behind him. Joshua took up the chase, yelling for his dog. Spooky, a white streak, darted behind the filling station. Sarah tried to catch Joshua who was well ahead of her. Peggy, dragging Amy, was last.

When they turned the corner of the building, Spooky, a tiny white dot in the distance, was running across a farmer's field, Frisky close behind.

"Look, Mama," said Sarah, "it's a cow pasture. Spooky's in a cow pasture!"

The rolling green field was dotted with black and white cows, several resting under a gigantic shade tree.

"That crazy cat!" exclaimed Joshua. "He's going to cause a stampede, just like in the cowboy movies!"

"It will be your dog's fault, Joshua. He's the one making all the noise."

"Look, look," added Amy. "Pooky's goin' up the tree." All watched silently as Spooky, never slowing, effortlessly climbed the tree and disappeared among the leafy branches.

"Get down there and get your dog," ordered his big sister.

Joshua started to climb the pasture fence, then hesitated. "Mama, do they look like wild cows to you?"

"Sarah," said her mother, taking charge, "take the car and go up to the farmhouse. See if there's anyone home that can help us. We need to be on our way as soon as possible."

Sarah hurried around the station and got in the car, yelling at the attendant. "My mama will pay you, sir!" She pulled out on the highway and turned down the first dirt road on the right, slowing the car only when she saw a plume of dust in the rear view mirror. Pulling up in front of the house, Sarah stepped on the front porch and knocked loudly on the screen door. She could hear footsteps and soon a man in bib overalls appeared.

"What can I do for you, little lady?" he asked kindly. Before Sarah could answer, he held the door open and invited her inside.

Speaking rapidly, Sarah introduced herself and explained the situation. She glanced around the room. There was a big radio beside a fireplace with a wide mantle. Every table held knickknacks and figurines. A dark red rug with big flowers covered the floor. Chairs and a sofa were covered in large flowered fabric. Sarah had never seen such a busy looking room.

The man smiled a slow smile. He held out an enormous hand and said, "It's nice to meet you, Sarah Bowers. My name's Mike Lawrence. Why don't you come on back in the kitchen and have some lunch. We got some mighty fine maypeas with little potatoes . . .

"Oh, no, sir, I can't. My mother and my brother and sister are waiting for me back at the station." Delicious odors from the kitchen made Sarah regret that she didn't have time to accept the kind man's invitation.

"Samuel," the man called. At that moment a tall young man appeared at the living room door. His mother followed, wiping her hands on her apron.

"Yes Sir?" he said, wearing a bored expression. When he saw Sarah his face brightened and he stepped across the room, holding out his hand. "I'm Samuel Lawrence."

Sarah noticed Samuel was as tall as his father and also wore bib overalls. Sarah didn't know when she had ever seen such dark brown eyes.

"Samuel, throw the ladder in the back of the truck and see if you can get her cat out of the tree." He turned to Sarah. "You're welcome to sit here with Janie and have a slice of apple pie while he fetches your cat."

The words 'apple pie' made Sarah's throat constrict. She realized it had been a long time since breakfast. "Thanks, but I need to get back to my family."

"I understand. Climb in the truck and you can ride with Samuel."

This suggestion seemed acceptable to Samuel, who couldn't take his eyes off their company.

"Come on," he said, smiling, "you can sit up front."

Sarah was relieved to learn she wouldn't be bouncing across the pasture in the back of a pick up truck. She climbed in the dusty red machine while Samuel loaded a stepladder. He looked over at Sarah and grinned. "Where are you from?' he asked.

"I'm from Raleigh, on my way to the coast to see my grandparents."

"The city, huh? I couldn't live there."

"Why not?" asked Sarah politely.

"You couldn't hear whippoorwills on summer evenings just before dark, or frogs sing after a hard rain."

Sarah stole a glance at Samuel's profile. She noticed he had blonde curly hair escaping from his straw hat, and a sprinkling of freckles across his nose. *Why can't he live in Beaufort,* she thought ruefully.

"I know how you feel. I'm used to living in the city, but when I grow up, I'm going to live near the ocean. All winter I miss the pelicans, shore birds and wild ponies that live along the salt marsh and the outer islands."

Samuel pulled the truck alongside the tree, careful to not disturb the cows. They seemed mildly curious at first, then continued chewing their cud, their eyes half closed. Sarah could see her family still standing by the fence. "Is it safe for them to walk across the pasture? The cows won't bother them, will they?"

"Long as they watch where they step, they'll be fine," said Samuel propping the ladder against the tree.

Sarah waved and watched as the others soon walked up. After introductions, Samuel turned to Joshua. "See if you can get your hands on that little dog. Every time I reach for his leash, he growls."

"Sure," said Joshua, sounding important. "I can control the dog."

"Oh, brother," muttered Sarah.

Samuel moved closer to Sarah, never taking his eyes from her. "I beg your pardon, Sarah. Did you say something?"

"Oh, no, Samuel," she replied, smiling. "I was thinking how kind it is of you to help us when I know you have other things you need to do."

"I'm more than glad to do anything I can for such a pretty girl."

"Thank you," replied Sarah, suddenly self-conscious.

A pitiful 'meow' was heard above. "Maybe we'd better try to get Spooky down, Sarah," suggested the mother.

"Yes, Ma'am, Miz Bowers. I'll have your cat down in a jiffy. I been climbing this tree since I was a little boy." With that, the handsome young man jammed his hat farther down on his head and climbed the ladder to the first limb. Swinging himself up, he caught the next limb. From the ground, all watched as Samuel approached the frightened cat. They could hear him talking softly, calming Spooky's fears. Soon, he scooped the cat up in his hands and began climbing down the tree. When he reached the ground, he handed the cat to Sarah as if it were a priceless treasure.

Sarah held firmly to her pet and smiled up at Samuel. As she did, she realized it was nice to talk to a boy taller than she. "I don't know how to thank you, Samuel. I was afraid I may never see Spooky again."

"It was my pleasure, Sarah. Uh, where did her get a name like 'Spooky'?"

"That's a long story. Maybe someday I'll have a chance to tell you."

The spell was broken when Amy announced, "I have to potty. I have to potty, now!"

Samuel laughed. "Everybody get in the truck, and we'll go back to the house. Miz Bowers, you ride up front with Sarah and me. Amy can sit in your lap and Joshua can ride in the back with his wild dog."

On the ride back to the farm house, Sarah sat close enough to Samuel for their shoulders to touch. She noticed the faint odor of soap mingled with the smell of hay. Sarah was fascinated by his lean brown arms and hands as he expertly steered the truck across the bumpy pasture.

When they reached the house, Samuel's parents were waiting on the porch. Sarah, still holding tightly to Spooky, introduced her mother, brother and sister. Amy was hurried into the house while the others waited on the porch.

"You folks might as well come on in and sample some of Janie's apple pie."

Before Peggy could refuse, Janie Lawrence said, "Nobody's ever refused a piece of my apple pie. My feelings are going to be hurt if you don't have a slice. Why, my recipe has taken first prize at the county fair three years in a row."

Soon, all were sitting around the table in the big farm kitchen. Oil cloth covered the table, soft cushions in each chair. Peggy watched Sarah and Samuel exchange glances, acting as if no one else was in the room.

When the last morsel had been scraped from the dish, Peggy announced, "We have to get on the road. My parents will be worried."

As they walked out to the car, Peggy thanked each of them again for their hospitality. Sarah and Samuel were standing together, speaking in low tones. "Come on Sarah," called Joshua. Reluctantly, she climbed under the wheel and started the engine. Samuel stood by the door.

"I'll write to you this summer," she promised. On the highway, Sarah turned to her mother. "Didn't you think he was cute, Mama?"

"He seems very nice, Sarah, and has lovely manners."

"He gave me his address, and we're going to write this summer. Maybe in the fall he'll come to the state fair."

"Sarah has a boy friend," sang a voice from the back seat. "He must be desperate if he wants to write to you."

"Just think, Mama. We could have tied Joshua to that big shade tree and left him there."

"Are we there?" asked Amy.

Peggy looked over her shoulder. "Read to your sister, Joshua," she said firmly.

"What do you want to hear, Amy," he asked wearily.

"Raggie Ann and Andy in the Deep, Deep Woods."

Joshua, martyred, opened the book, its pages worn from many readings. "Raggedy Ann and Andy were sitting under a tree in the deep, deep woods, filled with fairies n' everything, drinking a glass of soda water through two straws."

Soon the pets and Amy were napping peacefully. When they were several miles from the coast, the air rushing through the open windows began to change. No longer was the breeze hot and dry. Now the air was cool and damp. When they neared their destination, Peggy closed her eyes and breathed deeply. "I can smell the marsh, Sarah. I know I'm home."

At last the car came to a stop in front of her grandparents' stately Victorian home on Ann Street. Papa Tom and Granny Jewel rushed out to greet them.

"Oh, my gosh, Tom, look who's driving," shouted their grandmother. The back door of the car flew open. Joshua, Amy and the pets tumbled out and into the waiting arms of their grandparents. After hugs, Joshua rushed into the house to find Clara, knowing she'd be in the kitchen cooking a special treat. Papa Tom swung Amy up into his arms and followed. Granny Jewel, after hugging Sarah and exclaiming over how beautiful she was, linked arms with her daughter.

"How was the trip down, honey?"

"It was fine, Mama, just fine."

Sarah paused and watched them disappear in the house.

Hmmm, she thought, *even when you're forty you still don't tell your parent's everything.*

Chapter 2

"Clara, Clara!" shouted Joshua as he ran through his grandparents' stately home, his bare feet slapping against the hardwood floor. He paused and looked wistfully out the back screen door. "It's not going to be the same this summer without Little Chick."

Clara quickly dried her hands on the hem of her apron, walked over and put her hand on his shoulder. "He's not really gone, Joshua. Ramie moved him over to his house so his little hen wouldn't be lonely. He thought it was about time she had a boyfriend to keep her company." Clara smiled at the boy beside her. "Who knows? Maybe that no-account rooster will be a daddy someday and can strut around the yard cock-a-doodle-doin' so the whole world will know he's got chicks."

Joshua looked up. "Does he still limp?"

"Yes, but he's learned how to get around as good as any rooster."

Joshua continued staring through the screen door. "Just like Ramie," he said quietly.

"Um-hum, just like Ramie," replied Clara.

Suddenly, she whirled around. "Mercy, I'll never have breakfast ready for a hungry houseful if I stand here all day talking about that pitiful chicken that I should have fried up last summer."

Joshua grinned. "You don't mean that, Clara. You wouldn't cook Little Chick."

"Enough talk about that chicken," declared the cook. "Come here and give old Clara one of your bear hugs." Clara, the Mitchell's cook and housekeeper was more family than a hired domestic. She had come to work for the Mitchells' when Granny Jewel was a young bride.

After receiving a hug, Clara held the boy at arms length. "My, oh my," she said quietly, "how you have grown! You're practically a man!"

"That's right, Clara, I'm almost a man." He held up his arm and made a fist, causing a small bulge in his upper arm.

"Look who else is here," announced Papa Tom, carrying Amy.

"Cla-wa," said Amy, holding out her arms.

"Come here my baby," said Clara, embracing the child. "Clara made some fried potatoes for her girl. Would you like some?" Clara sat Amy on the counter and gave her a bowl of crisp, fried potatoes.

"Lord, lord, that sure is a pretty child," said Clara, looking at Amy's fair skin and blonde curls, still tousled from the trip.

"She takes after her grandfather, Clara. Don't you see the resemblance?"

Clara puffed out her cheeks. "Don't say such a thing! She's not going to go through life with your nose! Why, if she looks like you, even the pets won't play with her. When she goes out in the yard, the birds in the trees will fly away. If she looks like you, she won't be able to go fishing, 'cause she'll scare the fish off the hook. Even the . . ."

Tom Mitchell raised his hands. "Ok, Clara. You've made your point. If you look closely, you can see she resembles her Granny Jewel, especially around the eyes."

"Praise be," said Clara.

"I'm following my nose to the best cook in the world," rang another voice. Sarah stuck her head around the kitchen door. "Hello, Clara. I'm so glad to see you!"

Clara paused, dishcloth in hand. "Sarah, honey, is that you?" Clara's eyes misted over. "You're a woman! My baby girl is a woman!"

"Oh, Clara," she said, embracing the older woman she had always thought of as 'Aunt Clara. "I'll always be your little girl."

"Look," observed Joshua, "Sarah's taller than Clara." He looked at his grandfather. "Papa, does that mean Clara can't tell her what to do anymore?"

"No, son. "None of you will ever get that tall, or that old. I'm taller than Clara, and she bosses me around."

Clara's eyes narrowed. "Yes, and you need bossing. Who would keep you out of trouble if it wasn't for old Clara?"

"Goodness knows I try," said Granny Jewel stepping into the already crowded kitchen. "It takes both of us to keep your grandfather out of trouble." The grandmother stood on tiptoe and gave her husband a peck on the cheek.

Amy's face, smeared with ketchup, changed to a worried frown. Holding a fried potato in one hand, she asked, "Are you being a bad boy, Papa?"

"Every chance I get, sweetheart."

The zany conversation was interrupted by the ringing of the telephone.

"Law, I'll bet it's that boy calling here again. He calls every day wanting to know if Sarah's here. I can't get a thing done around this house for answering the telephone."

Clara's last words were unheard by Sarah as she dashed through the house. Picking up the receiver on the third ring, she said sweetly, "Hello."

"Sarah?" said a deep voice on the line. "Sarah, is that you? This is Bruce, Bruce McCoy. Can I come over tonight? I've waited nine months for this date." Both laughed, relieving the tension.

"I need to get unpacked and visit with my grandparents tonight."

"How about tomorrow?" Bruce offered. "Would you like to go sailing?" he asked hopefully. "I have a sailboat my grandfather gave me."

"I've never been sailing. My grandfather's boat has a motor."

"Sailing is nothing like that. I think you'll like it."

Sarah placed her hand over the receiver. "Mama," she called, "Bruce wants to take me sailing tomorrow. Will you need me?"

"No, honey," her mother called from the living room.

"Sure, Bruce, tell me what time, and I'll be ready."

They agreed on a time, and Sarah replaced the receiver. She stepped into the living room and joined the others who were enjoying a glass of Clara's lemonade.

"I've never been for a sailboat ride," said Joshua, sipping his icy drink. "I want to go, too." He looked at his sister, giving her his sorrowful look which usually got him whatever he wanted.

"Sorry, little brother, you're not invited," answered his sister.

"Mama!" he shouted, "make Sarah let me go! It's not fair for her to get to go boat riding and not me."

"Me too, me too," chimed Amy.

"Oh, this is wonderful," said Sarah sarcastically. "Let's *all* go. I know Bruce will be thrilled to have a boat load."

"Children!" said Peggy. "Let's settle this matter. Sarah has a date to go sailing tomorrow. No one else from this house will be going."

"How old is Bruce?" asked Papa Tom.

"Who are his parents?" asked Granny Jewel.

"Is he a good sailor?" asked their mother.

Sarah collapsed on the sofa and reached for an icy drink. "Papa Tom, Bruce wants to go to State College in Raleigh when he finishes high school." She turned to her grandmother. "His parents are Grace and Andrew McCoy. His father works at the Marine Corps Air Station at Cherry Point. They go to the Baptist Church."

Now she turned her attention to her mother. "Mama, he has sailed with his grandfather since he was a little boy. When his grandfather died last year, he left the boat to Bruce."

Papa Tom looked suspicious. "How do you happen to know so much about this boy?"

"Oh, Papa, we've been writing to each other every week the whole school year. I feel like I've known him forever."

"Hmmm," murmured Granny Jewel, "I know his mother. She's in the Women's Club. She's very nice."

"They're good customers, too. I remember seeing Alex, the grandfather, sailing Taylor's Creek with that little fellow."

Sarah asked wearily, "Does that mean it's safe for me to go?"

"Yes, honey," her mother replied. "He sounds like a fine boy."

Sarah finished her lemonade and went out to start unloading the car. *Hmmm,* she thought, *in a small town a person is judged by who his family is, not by who he is. In the city, a person is judged by who they are, because there's a good chance nobody knows the parents. I think I like it better that way,* she decided, carrying a suitcase in each hand.

Sarah sat the suitcases in the front hall. "I just thought of something," she said, addressing the whole family, "What should I wear tomorrow?"

Papa Tom spoke first. "You'll need some black rubber knee waders and a set of oil skins with a hood."

Sarah gave her grandfather a puzzled look. "What, Papa?"

Before Granny Jewel could stop him, he continued. "Sailors wear foul weather gear when they are on the high seas, especially during a winter storm. Why a person can freeze to the mast if they're not careful."

"Papa," said Sarah, becoming exasperated. "I don't think Taylor's Creek would be considered the 'high seas.' And," the girl continued, "I've never heard of a person freezing in June."

"Suit yourself, honey. I'm just trying to give you the benefit of my years of knowledge and experience."

Clara appeared to clear the table of empty glasses. "Humph, ask your grandpapa how he fared crossing the Atlantic Ocean in a troop ship during World War I."

Joshua's eyes widened. "Tell us Papa. Tell us what it was like." The boy, sitting on the sofa, inched closer to his beloved grandfather.

Looking uncomfortable, Papa Tom replied, "That was a long time ago. I can't seem to remember."

"Let's see if I can refresh your memory," said Clara, wearing a sly smile.

"It was about that time my mama and I were helping Miz. Mitchell do spring cleaning. She was worried sick about her boy, since Owen's mama had already gotten the news that she had lost her son on the battlefield. So, here comes a letter from your grandpapa telling his mama how terrible sick he'd been. She about passed out until she read some more and found out her boy had been sick alright,—*sea* sick." She turned to Joshua. "Your grandpapa got his knowledge and experience of the high seas by lying in his bunk the whole way across the ocean." Clara, triumphant, returned to the kitchen,

"Is that true, Papa?" asked a tiny voice.

"Your grandfather was saving his strength for fighting the enemy, which he did very well," Granny Jewel added smoothly.

Sarah sat on the other side of her grandfather. "Were you and Owen friends?" she asked quietly.

"Yes, Sarah. Owen and I grew up together and were best friends."

"Owen was Miss Nettie Blackwell's sweetheart," added Peggy.

"Didn't Owen's mama and Miss Nettie pray for his safety every day?"

"Yes, Sarah."

"Did you and great-granny Mitchell pray for Papa every day?"

"Of course. We prayed every day."

"Why did God answer your prayers, and not Miss Nettie's?"

The room grew silent. Finally, the grandmother spoke. "Owen and your grandfather were idealistic young men. They joined the army to do their part to combat evil. Young men have been doing this since before recorded history. Some are fallen heroes, others survive and return home. In war times, everyone makes sacrifices, some with their lives."

"When I get to Heaven that's the first question I'm going to ask," said Joshua.

"Me too," echoed his grandfather.

"Me too," agreed Amy, sitting in her mother's lap.

When Joshua, his mother and grandfather stepped out to finish unloading the car, Sarah turned to her grandmother. "Really, Granny Jewel, what does a girl wear on a first date if she's going sailing?"

The grandmother tapped her chin with one finger. "Let me see . . . In my day a girl would wear a long flowered skirt and ruffled blouse, and of course, a parasol to protect her delicate skin."

"Thanks, Granny Jewel."

Sarah walked back to her little bedroom behind the kitchen her grandparents fixed for her several summers before when it seemed she was too old to share a bedroom with her brother.

"Clara?" she asked, her hand on the doorknob, "What do you think I should wear on the sailboat?"

"Honey, you strap a life preserver around you just in case that boy capsizes the boat. I think your grandpapa has an old one he bought before the war. It don't look too good but it will work."

"But I can swim, Clara. Why do I need a life preserver?"

"You might fall overboard and hit your head and drown." Sarah remembered Clara was always sure there was a disaster around every corner. *Maybe I'll call Nancy and tell her I'm here so we can make some plans*, Sarah decided. *She should know what one wears when one is going sailing since she has an etiquette book for all occasions.*

"Hi, Nancy. It's me! I'm back for the summer."

"Sarah!" said Nancy Russert excitedly. "When did you get here? I'm coming around right now because there's so much I need to tell you."

A few minutes later, Nancy's gentle tap was heard on the front door.

"Come in," called Sarah. After Nancy had greeted everyone, the girls went back to Sarah's room.

"I just love this room, Sarah," said her friend. "It reminds me of a doll's house. The pink walls and pink flowered spread and curtains make it look like an illustration in a children's book."

"Sit while I unpack," said Sarah. "First, tell me what I should wear if I have a date to go sailing." Sarah, wearing a sly grin, looked at her friend.

"*What?*" exclaimed Nancy. "A date with who?"

Sarah, trying to look nonchalant, replied, "Bruce McCoy"

"You two didn't waste any time."

"Nancy, we've been waiting nine months. Last summer, as I was leaving for Raleigh, he asked if I was coming back so we could go on a date. Of course I promised I would. We've been writing to each other all year."

"Sarah, he's only one of the most popular boys at Beaufort High. Every girl in school wants to go out with him."

"Does that include you?" Sarah remembered Nancy's interest in her friend, Porter Mason, several summers ago. It was the only time Sarah was ever angry with her friend.

"No, silly. I have my own boyfriend."

Sarah felt relieved by this news. "Don't sit there looking so prim and proper, tell me all about him, every detail!"

The two girls sat on the edge of Sarah's bed. Nancy rolled her eyes and took a deep breath. "Well, one day I was on my way to English class when Henry Eubanks stopped me in the hall and asked if I'd go to the junior-senior prom with him. I was so excited! I couldn't concentrate on my studies the rest of the day. Thank goodness Mama didn't insist on making my dress. She let me go to Potter's Dress Shop and buy one! I can't wait for you to see it. I think you'll love it since it's pink."

"Tell me what he looks like."

Nancy closed her eyes and clasped her hands over her heart, a gesture Sarah remembered from other summers.

"He has curly brown hair, dark brown eyes, and grins all the time. He's always joking about something."

"Did you have fun at the prom?"

"We had a ball! The gym was decorated in crepe paper streamers and there was a live band. We danced every dance and really cut a rug when they played boogie woogie. Do you remember the summer we taught your Uncle Herb how to dance?"

Sarah nodded.

"Well, this was ten times more fun." Nancy dropped her voice to a whisper. "When he brought me home, he asked if he could give me a good night kiss. I said 'yes' right away before he lost his courage."

"Are you all still dating?"

"Yes! We have a date tonight."

"One question. Did your parents want to know who his parents were before you went out?"

"Sarah, honey," said Nancy, falling back on the bed, eyes on the ceiling, "the FBI has never searched a person's past like my parents."

Sarah fell on the bed, both girls bubbling with laughter.

When Sarah could catch her breath, she said, "You still haven't told me what I should wear tomorrow."

"Let's see," said Nancy, suddenly serious, "white sneakers, white slacks and a striped shirt. Pin your hair back on one side and wear sun glasses like movie stars."

"I don't have a striped shirt. Will a plaid one do?"

"Of course not! You need a knit shirt that will show off your figure. Forget baggy blouses, they're for kids."

"Let's go shopping," suggested Sarah.

Nancy frowned. "I can't stay long because I have to pack."

"Where are you going?"

Nancy looked excited. "I'm going to music camp in Greensboro for six weeks."

"When are you leaving?" asked Sarah disappointed.

"Tomorrow morning at six o'clock. I'm so excited. Just think, I'll be around other musicians who think nothing of practicing six hours a day. Here everyone thinks I'm crazy to spend so much time at the piano."

Sarah looked away quickly. She, too, had wondered many times why Nancy would willingly sit for hours practicing. "Come on," she said, changing the subject. "This won't take long. I'll buy the first pretty shirt we see."

"Where are you beautiful maidens off to in such a rush?" asked Papa Tom from behind his newspaper. He was sitting in the living room, feet propped on the coffee table.

"We're going shopping for a shirt, Papa Tom. I have to have something to wear when I go sailing."

A puzzled look came over the grandfather's face. "Didn't you just drag two huge suitcases back to your room? Wasn't there a shirt in either of them?"

Sarah patiently explained. "Yes, I have plenty of shirts, but none of them are right."

"I don't understand the female mind, but I want to give you the money."

"No, Papa. Mama will pay for it."

"Consider this a loan. Starting next week, I want you to work at the grocery store."

"That's great. I can buy my fall clothes at the end of the summer, just like last year."

"Last year was part time, this year I need you full time. Every year more and more visitors spend their summers in Beaufort and we stay real busy."

After the heat of the house, the shade from giant elms and the cool ocean breeze felt refreshing to the girls as they hurried to complete their mission.

Chapter 3

Sarah walked beside Bruce, matching his stride as they hurried toward Front Street.

"I left the boat tied to the Inlet Inn dock," he offered. "I get nervous if she's out of my sight too long."

Sarah wished she could think of something interesting or witty to say. *My cousin Marnie would be flirting and talking a mile a minute,* she thought with chagrin. Under her spell Bruce would be stumbling along, hanging on her every word, his boat forgotten.

When they turned the corner onto Front Street, Sarah glanced ahead and saw, tied to the end of the dock, the most beautiful white hull with a tall mast. The smooth sides, streamlined for speed, shone brightly against the blue-green water. She stopped and stared. "Bruce," she whispered, "is that your boat?"

He looked down and grinned. "Yep. That's my girl. Isn't she a beauty?"

"Oh, yes," Sarah agreed, no longer feeling at a loss for words.

"My granddaddy laid the keel and built her right in the back yard when daddy was about my age. She gets a fresh coat of paint and barnacles scraped off her bottom every year, so she's still like new."

Bruce stepped aboard and reached for Sarah's hand. "Have a seat in the stern while I shove off."

As soon as they cleared the dock, Bruce raised the sail which caught a puff of wind. The canvas, which had been flopping and lifeless, suddenly filled with air, growing taut. The streamlined craft, which had been bobbing in the water, now slipped effortlessly down Taylor's Creek.

"Sit by me," said Bruce, "and I'll give you some pointers on sailing."

"I already know a lot about boats," said Sarah. "I've been out many times with my grandfather." Sarah didn't want this handsome boy to think she was ignorant of boats, even if she was from Raleigh.

"It's not the same, Sarah," he explained. "Using a motor, or rowing a boat doesn't take the skill or effort needed for sailing."

I'm not going to argue, thought Sarah, *but if he thinks rowing a boat takes no effort, he needs to think again.* She answered him with a sweet smile.

Bruce turned the boat east, and sailed down the middle of Taylor's Creek as the sail filled with a fresh breeze from the south. Sarah leaned against the side of the boat, feeling herself relax. "This is fun, Bruce. We don't have to hear the whine of the motor, and we don't have to use oars."

"That's right. We'll let the wind do all the work."

For a few moments, neither spoke. It was enough to hear water rushing past the hull, and the cry of shore birds overhead.

"Have you decided what you're going to do after you graduate?" asked Sarah when the silence became awkward.

Bruce, holding the tiller, looked over at Sarah. "Yeah, I've thought about it, and I think I want to be a math teacher. I know I'll never get rich," he said smiling, "but it bothers me that so many students struggle with math, especially algebra."

Oh, brother, thought Sarah, *he must have seen my report card.*

"I want to do something useful with my life. If I'm drafted, then I'll serve my country for two years in the military, but I don't want that to be my career. If I have a degree in math, I can get a job anywhere in the United States or even a foreign country. I've never been anywhere, and I'd like to travel." He studied the sail for a moment, and tightened a line, the craft immediately answering his gentle touch. He reached over and placed a hand over Sarah's. "Most of all, I want to see the students' faces light up when they understand a concept they were struggling with."

"If you're a teacher, you have to grade papers every night."

"I don't think I'll mind that. I grade papers for the freshman math teacher and it's not too bad."

"My Aunt Miriam is a high school teacher."

"I'm going to have her for senior English this year. I'm looking forward to it because everybody loves being in her class." The boy gave Sarah a broad wink. "Maybe you could put in a good word for me." Bruce laughed, "I'm going to need all the help I can get. Writing term papers is not my idea of fun."

"Hey, I'm doing all the talking. How about you, Sarah? What are your plans after high school?" She glanced at the boy and saw him staring, waiting for an answer. She thought about her friend Nancy who dedicated most of every day to becoming more skilled as a musician. Her friend Lindsay, who lived in Raleigh was thinking seriously about going to nursing school. "I want to help people who are suffering," she told Sarah.

"I'm not *real* sure," she hedged. "I'm still trying to decide. I may want to study business since I'm pretty good at typing. Raleigh has two business colleges. My mother quit college to marry my father, and I think she's always been sorry she didn't finish."

The tide was 'dead low' and soon would turn and begin coming in. Sarah looked out over the marshes and mud flats, watching shore birds dip their bills in tidal pools, searching for minnows. *Everybody knows what they want to do with their life but me.* She looked over the side of the boat. *Even the tide knows what it's going to do.*

"Hey, you look like you're a million miles away, Sarah, penny for your thoughts."

Suddenly, it seemed easy to talk to the handsome, brown haired boy sitting beside her. "Bruce, I don't *really* know. All my friends are pretty sure what they want to do with their lives, and I worry sometimes that I'll finish high school and still not know."

"Have you prayed about it? Whenever I have to make an important decision, I pray first. I ask God to give me wisdom and guide me along the right path."

Sarah looked deep into Bruce's brown eyes, no longer self-conscious.

"That's exactly what I'll do. I'll pray every night until I have my answer."

"You don't have to wait until tonight. God listens to prayers all day, too. When I'm sailing, I feel as close to God as I do in church. The only difference is, out here I pray with my eyes open. The last time I closed my eyes to pray, I ran the boat up on a shoal."

"Did that interrupt your prayer?"

"Nope. It just changed. I started praying that God would release 'Willa' and me from the sandy bottom."

"I like the name Willa. Where did it come from?"

"Willa was my grandmother's name. There's a cute story of how my grandparents met."

"Please tell me," implored Sarah, sitting closer to the boy she had already come to think of as a friend.

Several minutes passed as Bruce adjusted lines and sheeted in the sail. Soon, he looked at Sarah and smiled. "My granddaddy lived on Harker's Island and the only way he could get to Beaufort was by boat. One summer morning he was sailing right down this same creek and spied a young girl sitting on the end of her daddy's dock, drying her long curly blonde hair in the warm sun. She was wearing a soft white dress and swinging her bare feet as she sang a song she learned in church. My granddaddy said right then he lost his heart just as if it fell overboard and got ate up by a barracuda. He dropped the sail on his little sharpie, grabbed a poling oar, and managed to guide the boat right up to the dock."

'How do you do?' he asked the beautiful girl using his very best manners. "My name is Alex Lewis, and I don't want to seem too forward, but I think I'm in love with you."

Bruce laughed. "When my granny smiled, and tossed her hair, my granddaddy's fate was sealed. But before he could tie the boat to the dock, he tore his eyes away from her long enough to see her daddy coming toward the dock, full throttle, his face looking like a thunder storm.

Bruce took a deep breath and grinned at his companion. "Grandaddy said he'd never been so scared before or since, as he was that day. There he was clinging to the dock piling, refusing to leave."

'Hey, boy, what business do you have with my daughter?' the huge man asked. Granddaddy said her daddy stood looking down at him, his feet spread apart and hands balled up in a fist.

"Grandaddy said his mouth felt like a field of cotton, his knees like putty, but he held on to the dock. 'Sir,' he squeaked, 'I've come to ask permission to court your daughter.' Her daddy was still wearing a fearsome expression.

'You ain't never seen my daughter before. How do you know you want to come courtin?' Grandaddy took a deep breath and looked my great-grandfather in the eye. 'Because' he said, 'I fell in love with her the minute I laid eyes on her and I plan to ask her to marry me.'"

"All this time, Willa was peeping around her daddy, smiling at granddaddy, the sun on her curly, yellow hair making a halo around her head." 'Listen here, boy,' her daddy said, 'you go home for a week. If you still want to come courtin' you present yourself next Sunday afternoon and plan to stay for supper. I'll decide if you can come back when the evening's over.'

'Thank you, sir,' says Granddaddy, finding his voice. 'I'll be here first thing, Sunday afternoon.'

He pushed off from the dock and coasted out to the channel, moving on the incoming tide. Before he raised the sail, he saw the beautiful girl waving from the end of the dock. 'I don't know your name,' he called.

'Willa. Willa Jean Guthrie.'

'Will you marry me, Willa Jean?' Her answer was merry laughter, borne on the south breeze."

Bruce grew silent, remembering his grandparents. Finally Sarah asked, "That is a lovely story. How are you able to remember every detail?"

"Sarah, I've heard my grandfather tell that story over and over my whole life. My granny got prettier, and her daddy taller with every telling." Bruce smiled at Sarah. "I hope someday I'll meet a girl just like her."

Before he could say more, Sarah asked, "What happened then? Please don't leave me in suspense."

Bruce propped his feet on the gunwale and loosened a line. "Granddaddy said that was the longest week of his life. He wasn't good for nothin'. His mama was scared he'd come down sick, and she was right. He was love sick. He couldn't eat or sleep, and he swears he dropped ten pounds."

"Did he go courting?"

"Oh, yes. He showed up on Granny's doorstep after church with a bouquet of wild flowers he picked along the shore."

Now Sarah was really interested in this quaint love story. *If only Nancy were here, she could clasp her hands over her heart and roll her eyes.*

"What happened next?"

"Granddaddy wore his only suit, which was heavy wool, and it turned off to be a warm day. He said it felt like his clothes were made of prickly pears. While he was sitting in the living room, trying to be polite, he could feel sweat running in a river down his back."

Sarah laughed as a picture formed in her mind.

"Anyway, they courted all summer, and in the fall, when the wind shifted to the north and the mullet were running, they got married and soon built a little house on Gallants Channel in Beaufort." Bruce's expression saddened. "When he died last year, I lost my best friend."

"Did he have a heart attack?"

"It wasn't a heart attack. He died of a broken heart. It was like he couldn't live without Granny. He'd talk about her for hours, like she was when they were young, not old and worn out. One day, near the end, he told me I should be the one to have his boat, and maybe one day when I'm out sailing, I'd meet a girl like my granny."

Bruce looked steadily at Sarah as his last sentence died on his lips. Sarah looked away and discovered they had come to the end of the creek. In the distance she could see a part of the Outer Banks of North Carolina. "Are we going to sail out there," she asked.

"Not today, Sarah. I wouldn't want to upset your grandfather."

"My grandfather? How does he know where we are?"

"Doesn't he drive a truck with Mitchell's Grocery painted on the side?"

"Sure, but what does that have to do with it?"

"The store must have had a lot of deliveries on Front Street today, because it keeps popping up. Still, they don't seem to be in a big hurry. The truck is going about the same speed as the boat."

"He's spying on me!" Sarah exclaimed, unsure how this knowledge made her feel.

"It's all right. After today, Mr. Mitchell will know what a good sailor I am, and maybe he'll trust me to take you sailing again."

Thoughts of Papa Tom were forgotten when Bruce called, "Duck, Sarah, we're coming about!" Bruce jammed the tiller to one side, making the boat heel over. Sarah grabbed the gunwale and held on.

"What's happening? Are we about to sink?" she yelled.

"Not today. We're just coming about," called Bruce, setting the sail at a new angle.

"About what?" she asked, still frightened.

In a single moment, the boat spun, the bow now facing in the opposite direction. Suddenly the sail, which had been taut, began luffing in the summer breeze, the boat barely moving. When he once again pulled the lines tight, the boat leaped through the water. Now it was pointed toward the opposite shore, and moving at a fast clip.

"Bruce, why is the boat pointed toward land? Aren't we supposed to be in the middle of the channel?"

Bruce, his attention on the boat, said, "The tide and wind are against us on the trip back to town. We're going to have to tack."

"Tack? How do you do that?"

"Sit tight and I'll show you," he said through clenched teeth.

Sarah watched in fascination as the shore rushed toward them. They were heading toward a dock with a boat tied alongside. When it seemed they were close enough to step ashore, Sarah closed her eyes and waited for the jolt, and the sound of splintering wood.

"Keep your head down, Sarah, we're coming about." Instantly, the boat changed direction and heeled over on her opposite side.

The girl dared to open her eyes and saw the opposite shore rapidly approaching. "What happened, Bruce?"

The boy, eyes bright and wearing a grin, replied, "We're on a different tack, Sarah. It's a zig-zag pattern that will get us back home."

"Are you sure? Why can't we sail down the creek like before?"

Bruce answered patiently, "The tide is against us and the wind, too. We have to sail into the wind and the only way we can do that is to tack."

Sarah noticed the shore was once again looming straight ahead. *I can't let him think I'm helpless*, she thought. "OK," she said, "what can I do? You seem to have your hands full and I want to help." Sarah continued to cling to the side of the boat as it tipped. Gone was the leisurely sail down Taylor's Creek she had enjoyed earlier.

Bruce gave her an admiring look. "Sure, you can man the tiller. When I say 'coming about,' you turn it the opposite direction and duck your head. If you don't, the boom will swing across and could hit you. People have been knocked out or knocked overboard from a boom."

"If we go out again," Sarah asked shyly, "would you like to borrow my grandfather's motor boat?"

Bruce didn't speak until they were on another tack. While there was nothing to do for several minutes, he replied, "Sailing is what I love. When my grandfather was young he couldn't clamp a loud stinky motor on the stern of his boat if the going got tough. Sailing is something that gets in your blood. If you have a streamlined boat that slips through the water, and responds to your lightest touch, you feel she's a part of you."

"I think I understand what you're saying, Bruce. Papa Tom loves his little boat, but spends most of his time saying really bad things to his motor."

Soon the stores of downtown Beaufort came into view. Now Sarah was enjoying the rhythm and challenge of sailing. When the bow was once again pointed toward Carrot Island, Sarah saw an area that looked familiar. She remembered the summer before when the townspeople rushed across the channel to rescue a foal that was hopelessly stuck in the mud. Without help, it would have died. She turned to Bruce, "Last summer, my grandfather helped rescue a . . . ."

Forgetting Bruce's warning, she sat up to get a better look. The boom swung across, soundly smacking Sarah on the back of her head. Like a rag doll, she collapsed in the bottom of the boat. Somewhere, in the distance she could hear Bruce calling. "Sarah, Sarah," in an agonizing tone. "Open your eyes and look at me!"

Slowly, Sarah eased one eyelid open. She heard a great roaring along with the most awful headache she had ever experienced. "Ohhh," she moaned. "I think I'm killed!"

Bruce tore off his shirt, soaked it in cool salt water and wrung it out making a compress for the newly formed goose egg on the back of her head. The boat, with no one at the helm and sheets loose, merrily floated back down the creek. "Lie down in the bottom of the boat, and I'll sail her on in. Keep talking to me so I'll know you're conscious."

Once more with tiller in hand and lines taut, Bruce regained the distance they had lost. "Say something, Sarah. Please don't be unconscious!"

"I'm OK, Bruce, it's just my head that hurts." Sarah's head hurt so badly, she wished she were Amy's age so she could crawl up in her mother's lap and wail.

Soon, Sarah heard the canvas of the mainsail drop to the bottom of the boat and she knew they were at the dock. It took all her strength to open her eyes and sit up. Bruce had already tied the *Willa* to a piling and was getting back in the boat. "Let me help you," he offered.

"No, no, I'm fine," Sarah assured him. Slowly, she crawled from the boat onto the dock and stood, trying to regain her balance. She felt sorry for Bruce, because she had never seen such a worried expression.

By the time they reached home, Sarah was feeling stronger. At the front door, she thanked Bruce for the boat ride. "You will go with me again, won't you?" he asked, almost begging.

"Sure, I'll be glad to go sailing again. It was a lot of fun until I raised my head."

"You may not believe me, but that happens to most sailors, *once*. After that, they remember to keep their head down."

Sarah was relieved when the boy left. *All I want is to lie down and rest my head.* She walked through the dining room as the family was finishing lunch.

"Hi, Sweetheart," called her mother. "How was your boat trip?"

Sarah looked at all the expectant faces. Her head started throbbing again and she suddenly remembered her grandfather's grocery truck following them along Front Street. Sarah remembered how angry it made her feel when she saw it. Ugly words tumbled from her lips. "I hope you got an eye full, Papa, spying on us! I have never been so embarrassed in my life! I'm sixteen, and too old for someone to watch everything I do." Close to tears, she hurried to her room and gratefully sank down on the bed, the soft white pillow cradling her aching head. She put one arm over her eyes to shut out the glare and felt tears trickle across the bridge of her nose and disappear on her pillow.

The door of her bedroom opened quietly. With some effort, she raised her arm and opened one eye. Clara stood beside her bed. "What is it, Clara?" she asked weakly.

After a moment, the woman spoke. "Why did you want to go and break your Papa's heart, talking to him like that? You know your granddaddy would never do anything to hurt you or anybody else in this family. He loves you better than life."

Sarah raised her voice. "I guess it's all right for you to talk awful to him, but I can't. What's the difference?" She turned over and faced the wall.

"The difference is, dear child, your Papa and I have been carrying on like that since way before your mama was born. If he ever stopped teasing me, I'd know something was wrong. I could hear your hurtful words all the way in the kitchen."

It was on the tip of Sarah's tongue to tell Clara to mind her own business, but she knew better. Without warning, tears came faster and faster. She was able to hide them until a sob caught in her throat. Instantly, Clara's attitude changed. "What's got you so upset, honey," she asked in a soft voice. "I knew that wasn't my girl talking out there. You can tell old Clara."

Before Sarah could speak, Clara continued, "Has that no-account boy done something to my child? If he has, I'll march right over to his house and knock him out with my stirring spoon."

Sarah was laughing and crying at the same time. "No, no, Clara," she finally managed. "Bruce is real nice, and I hope he'll ask me out again. It's just that I was so embarrassed when I realized Papa was following us along the street in the grocery truck. He shouldn't have done that." Sarah sat up and Clara put a protective arm around her. "He should trust me enough to know I'm not going to do anything wrong."

Clara gave Sarah a squeeze. "It wasn't you he didn't trust. For the first time, out there on that water, his grandaughter's safety was in someone else's hands. I guess he just couldn't help making sure you were safe. He's got to get used to the idea of another man in your life."

"No one will ever take Papa's place in my life, Clara, I don't care how many boys I date."

"Well, Missy, maybe you'd better go tell him. He's mighty unhappy right now, wondering what he did to hurt you so. He's guilty, there no doubt, guilty of loving his grand young'un too much."

Sarah managed a shaky grin. "I think I understand, now. Mama always says when I have children of my own, I'll know."

"Your pretty mama is a wise woman. Now, why don't you go out there and make peace with your Papa."

Sarah stood. "I will, Clara, and thanks." Sarah put her hand on the door knob, paused and turned. "Clara, did you know you can see stars in the daytime?"

"Stars only come out at night," Clara replied matter-of-factly.

"Well, I saw stars today circling around my head."

Clara frowned. "That boy better not be kissing you."

Sarah laughed. "No, Clara! I got hit on the head by the boom."

"Phew," said Clara, fanning her apron. "For a minute I thought it was something serious."

Chapter 4

On Sunday morning Sarah got up early so she might claim the bathroom before the rest of the family. She studied the face in the bathroom mirror and decided something serious had to be done about her hair. It had been droopy long enough. I couldn't roll it on bobby pins last night because my head hurt. Now my hair looks like a limp dish rag. When she got back to her room, she sat down at her vanity mirror and began to braid her long hair. She fastened the braids in a coil on the back of her head, being careful near the sore area. She slipped a soft cotton dress over her head and put on lipstick and powder. When she was satisfied, she went into the kitchen and set the table. Cereal, toast and juice were the Sunday morning menu since Clara wasn't there. After church, she would stop in to serve Sunday dinner. Cold fried chicken, potato salad and fruit waited in the refrigerator.

The family walked three short blocks to St. Paul's Episcopal Church. Papa Tom and Granny Jewel sang in the choir at the eleven o'clock service. Peggy, Joshua and Sarah sat in the congregation while Amy played in the nursery.

Sarah was happy to once more see the girls in her class. The only one missing was Nancy, who was attending music camp. "Welcome,

Sarah," said Mrs. Rogers, the teacher. "We have missed you. Are you staying with your grandparents?"

"Yes, Ma'am, we'll be here until Labor Day."

Bitsy Brooks leaned across Paula Jones and whispered, "I heard you had a date with Bruce McCoy."

Sarah smiled, "Yes, we went sailing. It was a lot of fun."

"Getting a bump on the head couldn't have been much fun." The girls looked expectantly, waiting for an answer.

How can they know what happened? wondered Sarah. *I didn't even tell my mother, for fear she would forbid me to ever go sailing again.* "How did you know?" Sarah questioned.

Bitsy looked mildly surprised. "Oh, everybody knows. Bruce told my boyfriend, Donnie, and he told me. Now, everybody knows." Sarah realized again how close-knit and caring people were in a small town. Before the girls could continue, Ada Rogers began the lesson.

After class, Paula asked, "Why don't you sing in the junior choir today. Some of our members are gone for the summer, and we could use the help."

"Thanks," replied Sarah, "but I didn't go to choir practice this week."

"The adult choir is singing the anthem, so we'll only be singing hymns."

Sarah gladly followed the other young people into the choir room. Sitting in the choir loft would be preferable to sitting next to her squirmy brother.

From her seat in the choir loft, Sarah looked about the fine old church. The dark, wooden rafters overhead resembled the ribs of a ship, since the carpenters who built the ships coming to America, also built the church. Stained glass windows gave the church a cool, rosy look, even on a hot summer day. There were cardboard fans in every pew to keep air moving during the service.

Bitsy nudged Sarah and passed a note written on the bulletin's margin. "Is Nancy going to write to you? I wonder if she's homesick."

Sarah looked across at the adult choir loft to see if her grandmother was watching. Relieved that she was concentrating on the minister's sermon, she wrote, "No, I don't think she misses anyone. She's staring at the keyboard all day."

Bitsy smiled and put the bulletin inside her hymnal.

Lunch was almost over when the telephone rang. Sarah hurried to answer it. "I don't remember Sarah being so enthusiastic about answering the phone last summer," observed her grandfather.

"She probably thinks that boy is going to call her," said Joshua. "Papa, do you think she bosses him around like she does me?"

"No, Joshua, not yet. However, the day may come when she gives him orders." Tom Mitchell dropped the subject when he saw the look his wife was giving him.

"That was Bruce," declared Sarah when she returned to the table. Before she could pick up a piece of crisp, fried chicken, Granny Jewel asked, "How is your head, Sarah? You neglected to tell us you had an accident in the boat yesterday."

All eyes were on the girl. "It was nothing. The boom tapped me on the head when we were coming about."

"It might be too dangerous to go sailing with Bruce," added her mother.

"Oh, Mama! Sailing isn't any more dangerous than walking downtown. I just have to remember to keep my head down."

"She's right, Peggy," said her father. "Sailing is a safe pastime as long as you remember when to duck." Sarah shot her grandfather a grateful look.

"Mama, Bruce wants me to go to church with him tonight. The youth have the service and he's going to deliver the sermon."

"That's fine, honey. Don't be too late. Your grandfather is putting you to work early in the morning."

Sarah thought she had just closed her eyes when she heard her grandfather's voice. "Rise and shine, Sarah Bowers! Today you join the working folks."

Sarah groaned and sat up in bed. Between Mr. Peavy on Broad Street, and her grandfather's cheerful voice in the next room, she knew there was no chance of catching a few more winks.

Sarah pushed back the sheet, noting that already the room was hot and stuffy. *It must be a hundred degrees in here. I'll go to the hardware store on my lunch break and see if Mr. Clawson has an electric fan. If so, I'll buy one when I get paid Friday.*

Once again Sarah braided her hair and wore it in a coil on the back of her neck. It felt so much cooler to have her hair up. She noted with relief that her head was no longer sore.

The two ate breakfast alone, the rest of the family still asleep. "Clara will be here any minute to fix breakfast for the rest of the family," said Papa Tom, buttering a piece of toast. He looked across the table. "You are going to be a big help this summer, honey. I haven't had time to tell you, but Kevin is going to work at the Marine Corps Air Station at Cherry Point. This is his last week at the grocery store." Papa Tom looked sad as he stirred his coffee. "We sure are going to miss him. He's been like part of the family."

Sarah felt a pang of disappointment. Kevin was grown, but still young enough to be fun.

Papa Tom looked at his watch. "We need to leave as soon as you're ready."

"I want to put on some makeup," said Sarah, getting up from the table.

"Don't put on too much paint, or the Beaufort boys will be falling all over each other just to get a glimpse of my granddaughter."

Sarah grinned, "You're silly, Papa."

Tom Mitchell looked at his granddaughter's beautiful chestnut hair, gray eyes and rose bud lips, and knew he was not being silly.

Mr. Case gave Sarah a bear hug. "Welcome back, gorgeous," he said. "Now business will be better than ever." Kevin, the tall sandy-haired clerk with a wide grin, also welcomed Sarah.

"Where is Uncle Herb?" asked Sarah, looking around the store.

"He comes in later, and stays late to close the store in the evening," explained Kevin.

Sarah remembered where the aprons were stored. She went in the tiny office and opened a cabinet. Inside was a stack of starched white aprons. She wrapped the ties around her waist twice, and tied them in front. "I feel like I never left," she told Mr. Case.

After walking the aisles and checking produce, Sarah paused at the office door, "It's as I remembered. Nothing's changed, even the prices are the same."

"That's competition, Sarah. If we suddenly raised prices, our customers would soon be shopping at City Grocery or C.D. Jones Co."

Sarah leaned on the door facing, her hands in the deep apron pockets. "How about if you were the only grocery store in town?"

"Then we'd have a monopoly on food prices," said Papa Tom.

"You could charge any price you wanted to."

"That wouldn't be ethical, my girl."

"I know, Papa. You would never take advantage of people." Before her grandfather could answer, the screen door slammed.

"Where is the pin up girl?" a voice boomed.

"Hello, Uncle Herb," said Sarah. Herb Mitchell swept his niece up in his arms. "Look at you," he exclaimed. "I didn't think it was possible, but you're prettier that ever." Before Sarah could respond, he asked," How are your cute mama and your brother and sister?"

"Everybody's fine, Uncle Herb. How is Miriam? Is she glad school is over?"

"I think she is ready to take it easy for a few weeks. However, we are looking for a house because the apartment is getting too small. If we find something, she'll be busy packing and decorating."

The screen door opened again, causing the tiny bell to tinkle and announce the first customer of the day. Sarah walked toward the front of the store and was surprised to see Bruce standing near the check out counter. "May I help you?" she asked graciously.

"Hello, Sarah," he said quietly, never taking his eyes from the girl. "I stopped in for a Coca-Cola, and to ask you if we could have lunch together."

The three men in the rear of the store smiled and let Sarah wait on the tall, handsome customer.

"I need to run two errands, Bruce. I don't know if I'll have time."

"How about tomorrow? We could bring a bag lunch and eat on the Inlet Inn dock."

"That would be fun," said Sarah, smiling.

"Be sure and bring some extra bread for the gulls," said Bruce, slowly backing out of the store. Reluctant to leave, he said, "I'd better go, or I'll be late for work."

When Bruce disappeared from view, Sarah turned slowly and saw four pairs of eyes staring. She set her mouth in a thin line and put her hands on her hips, as she had seen her mother and grandmother do many times. Quickly, all four turned to jobs that required their immediate attention.

The beauty parlor smelled the same as the summer before when she had her hair styled and curled. It was not an unpleasant odor, just one

44

all beauty parlors seemed to have. The receptionist greeted Sarah with a smile. "May I help you?"

"Yes, please," answered Sarah. "I need a hair cut and a cold wave."

"What's a good day for you?" asked the pretty girl with lacquered nails and matching lipstick.

"I don't have to work on Saturday," offered Sarah.

The girl studied the weekly schedule. "Emily can take you at nine o'clock Saturday," the girl answered. "What is your name?"

"Her name is Sarah," answered a musical voice. "She's one of my favorite customers, even if it's once a year."

To Sarah's delight, the girl she had most admired in the shop, stood before her. "Emily, I almost didn't know you. You look different."

Emily threw back her head and laughed. Sarah recognized her musical laughter at once. "Honey," she said, "Emily has a new look."

It was true. The Emily Sarah remembered from past summers had bright, blonde curls swept up on the top of her head, tied with a silk scarf that bounced and quivered when she walked. Gone was the bright red lipstick and chewing gum. Her hair was dark blonde, curling softly around her face, her lips and nails, a soft pink. "I have a few minutes before my next customer. Come back to my booth and let's talk."

Sarah followed Emily, fascinated by the different stages of development in getting one's hair done. Some were being shampooed, others wearing round, rubber curlers, some being combed out and ready to leave. The most complicated operation was the permanent wave. The odor from the chemicals involved was the characteristic smell.

"Now, Sarah," said Emily, when they reached her booth, "sit here and let's talk about what you want done."

Their eyes locked through the large mirror. "Your hair looks great, Emily. I want mine shoulder length and curly. I want curly bangs, too."

"If it's shoulder length, it will still be long enough to sweep up if you're going to a formal dance, or if you just want to get it off your neck on a hot day. All the movie stars wear their hair that way."

Sarah smiled at Emily's reflection. "I'm not sure how many formal dances I will be attending this summer, but I love the idea of pinning it up."

When they had finished discussing Sarah's new hair style, Emily's customer still had not arrived. Emily lowered her voice and whispered to Sarah. She had to listen closely over the whine of several hair dryers. "Since you haven't been here long, you may not have heard my good news."

"What's that, Emily?" asked Sarah.

The beautician held out her left hand. She was wearing a small diamond ring. It glittered in the overhead lights. "Oh, Emily! You're getting married! Who is the lucky fellow?"

The older woman smiled brightly. "I'm sure you know him. He works at your grandfather's grocery store."

"Kevin? You're going to marry Kevin?" Sarah leaped from the chair and embraced Emily. "He is such a nice person, always laughing and teasing. My grandfather says he is a real good worker." Sarah's face saddened. "This is his last week at the store. We won't be seeing as much of him anymore."

"He's going to work at Cherry Point. He'll be making more money, and with me working, someday we'll be able to buy a house."

"Have you set a wedding date? What church will you be married in? Have you picked out your dress?" Sarah remembered how exciting her Uncle Herb's wedding had been the summer before.

"We're getting married at the preacher's house, not in the church. It will only be his parents and mine."

"Oh," said Sarah, disappointment in her voice. She was already thinking of what to wear to the wedding. Sarah brightened. "How about a shower? All brides need a shower to get the things they need to set up housekeeping."

Emily studied her hands. "There are no plans for a shower or any parties."

"Why not?"

"Well, no one has offered and probably no one would come."

Sarah stood and faced her friend. "You are too going to have a shower because I'm giving you one! We'll invite the whole town." Sarah's lips narrowed, much like her grandmother's.

"That's very sweet, Sarah," replied Emily.

"Everybody likes you, Emily. There's no reason why they wouldn't come."

"You're right. Everybody likes me at the beauty parlor, but nowhere else." Emily stared at Sarah. "You see, I have a not-so-good reputation. Last year I ran away with a man, and I've done some things I'm not very proud of. I'm sorry now, but it's too late."

Before Sarah could think of an argument, Emily's customer arrived. "We'll talk more Saturday," she said, waving goodbye.

Sarah was staring through the plate glass window in front of the grocery store. *More unwritten laws* she thought. *The world of adults is very complicated and the rules are not written down. If you're grown, you're supposed to automatically know them.*

"What are you staring at so intently?" asked Papa Tom. Sarah turned slowly.

"Papa, do you think it's right to hold something against a person if they're sorry for what they did?"

"Jesus said in order to be forgiven, we have to forgive."

"How about if a woman has a bad reputation, and other women don't want to have anything to do with her?"

"I'm going to give you the best advice I know."

"What is it, Papa?"

"Hang up your apron, go home, and ask your grandmother."

Sarah hugged her grandfather. "Thanks, Papa. I'll see you at supper."

"Let me know what happens," he said as Sarah disappeared through the back door of the store.

"Here's my dear child," rang Granny Jewel's voice as Sarah hurried up the sidewalk. Without even a hello, the girl started, "If a person makes a mistake, should people hold it against them?"

Sarah watched her grandmother's eyes become narrow slits and turned her head to one side. "You look thirsty, honey. How would you like a tall glass of lemonade?"

"Under the tree, in the swing?"

"Right! I'll get the glasses, and you put on some shorts so you can be comfortable."

A few minutes later, sipping the ice cold drink, Sarah told her grandmother of her conversation with Emily. "I told her I wanted to give her a shower. When I said we could invite all the ladies, she didn't think any of them would come because of her reputation." Sarah looked at her grandmother. "Is that true, Granny? Would people stay away?"

"Sarah, that is a very hard question to answer. There are people who might stay away, but I don't think any of them live in Beaufort."

Sarah took her granny's hand. "In the Bible, Mary Magdalene had a bad reputation, and so did the Samaritan woman at the well. Jesus loved them anyway. Remember the time . . ."

Before Sarah could finish, she was yanked to her feet and pulled across the yard, lemonade forgotten. When they got to the porch, the grandmother still had Sarah firmly by the hand.

"Clara, turn off the fire under supper. Sarah, go find your mother and meet us in the living room. I'll get paper and a pencil."

In less than three minutes, all were gathered, eyes on Granny Jewel. "Ladies, we are going to give a party! To be more exact, *Sarah* is going to give a party."

For a moment this information was met with silence. Peggy drew a deep breath. "How lovely, Sarah! It's time you learned some of the responsibilities of social life." She paused a minute. "What kind of party, and, will there be a guest of honor?"

"It's going to be a bridal shower, and there will be a guest of honor."

"I certainly hope it isn't one of your friends. You're far too young to consider matrimony."

"The party is for a friend, an older friend."

"Don't keep us in suspense any longer."

Sarah took a deep breath. "I want to give Emily a bridal shower because she's getting married and she doesn't have anything to keep house."

Peggy's eyes flew to her mother. "Do you mean Emily at the beauty parlor?"

"Of course, Peggy," said the grandmother.

"Wouldn't it be much better to have a welcome home party for Nancy Russert, since she's your age? She'll be back in a few weeks."

"I want Nancy and I to be the hostesses. She knows how to decorate and what kind of food to fix."

Clara, who had remained silent, spoke, "Don't bother fixing a lot of fancy food. I got a feeling most of your guests will never show." She got up, smoothing her apron.

"Why not, Clara?" asked Sarah, searching the older woman's face.

"I guess you gotta' learn sometime. Let your granny explain 'cause I need to get back in the kitchen."

"Is she talking about Emily's reputation, Granny Jewel?"

"Well, yes, and the fact that not all the ladies in Beaufort have the same things in common."

"They only need one thing in common, and that is to like Emily."

At that moment Joshua came in the back door, letting the screen door slam. "Mama!' he called.

"We're in the living room," Peggy answered. "Is anything wrong?"

"Mackie's being mean to me. He told me to go home."

Joshua collapsed in the nearest chair. "Why can't he be nice?"

"Mackie is going through a rough time, Joshua. His mother is very sick and can't get out of bed. Members of the Baptist church take supper there each night since she doesn't have strength to cook. Someone told me Mackie reads to her every afternoon to keep her mind off the pain."

"He could have told me that, instead of telling me to go home," said Joshua sadly.

"He'll come around after a few days. This is the way he handles the pain of knowing his mother won't be with them much longer," said Peggy. "You keep being a friend, no matter what."

"I'm thankful it's not you, Mama," said her son, climbing on her lap, long legs resting on the floor.

"I'm thankful, too," said Granny Jewel, all thoughts of the party forgotten.

Chapter 5

Clara was stirring a pot of grits, waiting for it to thicken when someone was heard stomping up the back porch steps. She watched as Mackie Fuller appeared on the other side of the screen door. "Where is Joshua?" he demanded.

Clara never stopped the smooth circular motion of her stirring spoon, "Good morning, Clara," she said. "How are you today?"

The large, heavy set boy on the other side of the door gave a snort. "Yeah," he said disgustedly. Mackie was wearing a pair of dungarees sorely in need of washing, and a shirt two sizes too small whose buttons were in danger of popping off. Long strands of hair hung in his eyes which he pushed back with his hand.

Clara turned the fire out under the grits and gave her full attention to the boy. "I said," began the woman, "Good morning, Clara. How are you today?"

Mackie could see Clara, one hand on her hip and the other armed with her long, wooden stirring spoon. More than once he had heard tales from Joshua about the kitchen utensil that sometimes doubled as a weapon.

Mackie swallowed. In a soft voice, he began again. "Good morning, Clara. How are you today?" The boy's voice was sincere, but his eyes never left the instrument in Clara's hand.

"Good morning to you, Mackie," she said. "I'm just fine, and thanks for asking. Joshua isn't up, so why don't you come in and wait for him?" Clara turned her attention to the pot of thick, creamy grits, once more stirring them gently. Mackie gave a sigh of relief when he saw the wooden spoon disappear in the pot. From the corner of her eye, Clara watched Mackie Fuller slowly advance. When he was close enough, he glanced in the pot.

"Is that grits you're fixing?" He asked, staring.

"Yes, it's grits. I can fix the best pot of grits in this town. There's never a lump, and every mouthful goes down swimming in hot, melted butter." Mackie stood, hanging on her every word, his tongue licking his upper lip.

"I'm dishing it up right now. Would you like a bowl?" asked Clara, scraping a large hunk of pale yellow butter in the pot.

Mackie tore his eyes from the slow boiling contents. "Heck no! I don't need somebody else's food. I ain't no charity case."

Clara expertly dipped a cup full of the steaming food into a large bowl. She thrust it at the boy. "Get yourself to the table and mind you don't burn your tongue or spill a single drop."

"Yes, Ma'am," said Mackie, hurrying to the next room, afraid Clara may change her mind. She slowly shook her head while pouring a glass of freshly squeezed orange juice for the hungry guest. Soon, the sound of metal against china could be heard. Mackie had the bowl tipped in order to get the last spoonful. "Thank you," he mumbled, wiping his mouth with the back of his hand.

"Use your napkin, Mackie," instructed Clara.

"No need. I already wiped my mouth."

"Now the back of your hand and arm will be sticky," added Clara.

"I'll wipe my arm on the inside of my shirt."

"Never mind," said Clara shaking her head. She returned to the kitchen to finish preparing breakfast.

Sarah stuck her head out of her bedroom door. "You're early, Clara. Papa and I are supposed to be gone by the time you get here."

Clara, scrambling eggs, replied. "You can't survive all day in that old store on cold cereal every morning. I decided you and your grandpapa needed a little something that will stick to your ribs."

"Was I dreaming, or did I hear you talking to someone?"

"You heard right. Master Mackie Fuller is dining in this morning." Clara smiled and pointed toward the dining room.

"To what do we owe the honor of his visit?"

"I think he's waiting for Joshua. In the meantime, he's having a bite to eat," whispered Clara.

Sarah poured a glass of orange juice and went into the dining room. "Good morning, Mackie. How are you today?"

Mackie looked up, his lips shiny from buttered toast. Remembering his manners, he replied, "Good morning Sarah. I'm fine."

"Who is this lad joining us at this early hour?" Papa Tom came into the room, smiling at Mackie.

"Good morning, Mr. Mitchell. How are you?"

Tom Mitchell made no effort to hide his surprise at Mackie's rare display of manners. "I'm just fine, Mackie. How are your parents?"

"Daddy's fine, but he works all the time. When he finishes at the hardware store, he eats supper and most nights is busy painting people's houses." The boy's expression suddenly changed. His voice was barely a whisper. "Mama ain't too good. Every day I think maybe she'll be stronger and get out of bed. And every day she's weaker. My aunt Mable is coming on the bus Friday to help out. I can take care of my mama, but Daddy says we need her. We'll be all right as long as she don't try to tell me what to do."

"Of course you can take care of your mama, Mackie. She's very lucky to have a son like you," said Papa Tom.

"Can I go upstairs and see if Joshua is up?"

"Sure. If he's still asleep, feel free to wake him."

Mackie shoved his chair back, wearing a grin. "That'll be fun!" He started to leave the room when he heard Clara clear her throat.

"Is there something you want to tell me, young man?" Mackie gave her a blank look. "I'll give you a hint. It has to do with appreciation for breakfast."

"Oh, yeah, thanks." He was gone before anyone could speak.

Joshua was startled when he opened his eyes and saw Mackie Fuller looming over him. For a moment, he had that dreadful hollow feeling he used to feel when they first met.

Mackie plopped down on the other bed.

"Is anything wrong?" asked Joshua tentatively.

"No, it's just that my mama wants to talk to you. She asked me to come over and get you, so get up."

"Do I have time for breakfast?" asked Joshua, almost afraid to ask. "Would you like something to eat?"

"No thanks. Clara fixed me some breakfast but I ain't eating here no more."

Joshua was shocked. "Why not?" he demanded.

"You have to use too d—many manners. It's not worth it." He turned to leave the room and paused at the door. "Hurry up," he ordered.

Joshua scrambled from his bed, quickly smoothing the covers. Bare feet hit the upstairs hall while he was tucking in his shirt. He caught up with Mackie at the foot of the stairs. "Do you want to sit with me while I eat?"

"No. I'll be on the back porch where I won't have to listen to all you mannerly people." He looked at Joshua. "Just be quick about it."

Joshua tore through his breakfast, asked to be excused and was gone.

"What do you think that's all about, Papa?" asked Sarah.

"I'm not sure. With Mackie, there's no telling."

The boys squeezed through the opening in the fence, Mackie with more difficulty than the summer before. "Tell your grandfather he needs to knock another paling off his fence. The opening is getting too small."

"It's because we're getting too big," replied Joshua, realizing after he said it, he had corrected Mackie Fuller. He waited for the blow that never came. *Phew*, he thought, *thank goodness Mackie's got a lot on his mind today.*

When they got to the back porch, he turned and grabbed Joshua by the shirt. "Look here now," he began, "my mama don't feel good. She wanted me to bring you over here cause she wants to talk to you. Don't you tell her I said a bad word in your house, or you'll be sorry."

Joshua was close enough to count freckles on Mackie's cheeks. He shook his head vigorously, promising to die with the information.

In the kitchen, Mackie motioned to Joshua to be quiet. "I'll see if Mama's awake," he said. "You stay here."

Joshua remained rooted to the spot while the boy tiptoed into his mother's bedroom. Although the house was much newer than his grandparents', it looked sad and neglected. There were dirty dishes on counter tops, grocery bags abandoned in a corner, canned goods waiting to be put in cabinets. In the silence, he could hear Mackie talking to his mother. *Can that possibly be Mackie*, wondered Joshua. The voice was soft and loving, one Joshua had never heard before. Soon the boy came to the door and motioned for Joshua to come in.

"Mama's awake and she's ready to talk to you. I'll wait for you on the back porch." He brushed past Joshua, gently closing the screen door behind him. For several moments Joshua stared at the bedroom door. Slowly he walked toward the dark opening.

A soft voice came from the darkness. When his eyes became adjusted to the light, he could see a tiny woman lying in bed, head and shoulders propped on pillows.

"Welcome, Joshua. Come closer."

"Yes, Ma'am," he whispered.

"I know it's dark, but I can rest better like this." She pointed to a chair next to the bed. "Please sit for a minute because there's something important I need to ask you."

Joshua slowly sat on the edge of a wooden, straight-backed chair. He had to wait for several minutes while Mrs. Fuller caught her breath. She reached a claw-like hand out and rested it on Joshua's arm. "You're the best friend Mackie ever had. I never worry when he's with you. I've seen a change in him since you've been coming each summer. He admires the things you say and do, and how you stand up for what you believe is right." Mrs. Fuller took a deep breath and paused for a moment, as if she were searching for the right words. "I'm not going to be here to see my son grow up. What I'm asking is, will you help look out for Mackie? Will you be his conscience and try to steer him along the right path? He'll listen to you."

When she paused, Joshua cleared his throat. "Yes, Ma'am," he managed to say. "I'll look out for Mackie any way I can." Realizing what an awesome responsibility it would be to be Mackie's conscience, Joshua added, "My sisters and I will do everything we can." He added, "My grandparents can help out when I'm in Raleigh."

The promise made, Mrs. Fuller sank back among the snow-white pillows, a weak smile playing across her lips. "It's going to require a lot of prayer."

"Yes, Ma'am."

She released Joshua's hand, weak from the effort of holding it. As the boy rose to leave, she whispered, "Ask Sarah to come over this afternoon, and bring the baby. I'd like to see them both."

"Yes, Ma'am," Joshua repeated, slowly backing from the room. Once out in the sunlit kitchen, he drew a deep breath and hurried out to the back porch.

Mackie was sitting on the top step, head in hands. He looked up when he heard the screen door close softly. Joshua sat down beside him. "Do you think my mama's gonna die?" Before Joshua could answer, he made a fist with both hands. "You better tell me the truth or I'll pound you good."

Joshua stood. "I always tell the truth, Mackie, because I know you should, and I know what happens if I get caught in a lie." In a nearby tree a blue jay was scolding a squirrel. Joshua watched the drama for a moment. Finally, he turned to his friend. "Yeah, Mackie," he said softly. "I think your mama's gonna die."

Without warning, the older boy burst into tears, clamping both hands over his face to try and stem the flow of tears. "I don't know what to do without my mama! Ain't nobody gonna love me when she's gone!"

Joshua sat beside his friend. "No, Mackie, there are plenty more people. Your daddy loves you, and your Aunt Mable, and, and," Joshua paused, searching, "and my *whole* family loves you."

Mackie wiped his tear stained face with the front of his shirt and turned to his friend. "If you *ever* I mean *ever*, tell anybody that you saw me cry . . . ."

"Hush now, Mackie," whispered Joshua, daring to put his hand on Mackie's shoulder. "I'm not going to tell anybody, ever. I'm your friend."

When Sarah came home at four o'clock, Joshua was waiting for her on the front steps. "Sarah, Mackie's mama wants you to come over, and bring Amy."

"Why?" asked the big sister.

"She wants to see you, and I told her you'd come over after work."

Sarah thought for a moment. "I'll get Amy and go before supper. Maybe I'd better check with Granny Jewel, too. She may have something I can take over for their supper."

With a bag of oranges in one hand and Amy's hand in the other, the two sisters hurried along the sidewalk. Even at four o'clock the day's heat showed no sign of lessening. "Hurry along, Amy. We'll cook if we stay out here much longer." Amy's short legs could hardly keep up with her sister's long ones.

It was a relief to step on the Fuller's front porch. Sarah tapped gently on the screen door. "Yoo-hoo," she called softly, and soon heard footsteps coming from the back of the house. Mackie appeared at the door. "Hello," greeted Sarah. "We came to visit your mama. Does she feel like having company?"

"She's awake," mumbled Mackie as he took the bag of oranges. "Thanks for the fruit," he said walking toward the kitchen. Sarah and Amy stood awkwardly, waiting for his return. When he returned, he said, "She's feeling better since she took some pain medicine, so it's all right for you all to go in. She said she's been waiting for you."

Sarah scooped Amy in her arms and followed the boy into the darkened room. Once more Mrs. Fuller was sitting up in bed with pillows at her back. "Mackie, honey, raise the shade so I can see these pretty girls," she whispered. The shaft of light from the late afternoon sun shattered the gloom. "Come sit by me so I can see you."

Sarah sat in the same chair her brother had occupied earlier. To make conversation, Sarah began telling of all the customers she had met at the grocery store and her sailing adventure all the while holding Amy firmly in her lap.

"Today I gave your brother a big responsibility."

"What was that, Mrs. Fuller?" asked Sarah, trying to picture her little brother assuming a responsible role for anything.

"I asked him to look out for Mackie when I'm gone." She paused, then continued, "It is a big job for such a young fellow, but I know he can do it since Mackie admires Joshua. However, I want to ask you to help him if necessary."

"Me too," interrupted Amy.

"Yes, dear, you too."

Sarah's answer was much like her brother's. "We'll be glad to help any way we can, and I know my grandparents will always be there for Mackie if he needs them."

"I feel very much at peace now. Thank you for coming." Her eyes closed, and Sarah knew by her breathing the woman was asleep.

"Be very quiet, Amy. We don't want to wake up Mackie's mama," whispered Sarah as they left the room.

Mackie, eating an orange at the kitchen table, thanked them for coming.

Outside, they had to blink until their eyes became accustomed to the bright afternoon sun. "Come on, Amy, let's go home and help Clara. Maybe she'll let us set the table." Along the way, Amy spotted a late blooming dandelion and stopped to pick it. She sat down on the soft grass to blow the silvery seeds from the stem. Sarah sat beside her, enjoying the shade from a nearby tree.

"Sarah," the young child asked, never looking up, "can angels talk?"

"In the Bible the angel Gabriel talked and angels sang when Jesus was born. There's even an angel choir in Heaven. Our grandparents say they are going to join when they get there." Sarah smiled down at the soft, blonde curls of her little sister, still laboring to blow every seed from the dandelion. After a few minutes, she said, "Come on little sister. We don't want to be late."

Without moving, Amy asked, "Why didn't the angel talk today?"

Sarah moved closer to her sister. "What did you say, Amy?" she asked softly.

"I said, why didn't the angel talk?"

"What angel?"

Amy grew impatient with her older sister. She tossed away the used dandelion and looked up at her beloved sister. "You know, the angel standing beside the bed."

"I didn't see an angel."

"I did."

"What did he look like?"

"He looked the way all angels look."

"Oh."

Amy, still no longer, scrambled to her feet, Sarah close behind. Nothing else was said about their visit until all were seated at dinner. After the blessing, while Granny Jewel was passing bowls of hot stew and green vegetables, Sarah looked at her sister. "Tell the family about our visit, Amy."

Amy, carefully pushing green beans to the edge of her plate, looked at her mother. "We went to see a sick lady."

"Oh, "said her mother. "Did you have a nice visit?"

Amy, unused to having everyone's attention, launched into a detailed description of her afternoon.

When it looked as if Amy wasn't going to mention the angel, Sarah asked, "Was anyone else in the room, Amy?"

All waited until the little sister swallowed a mouthful of creamed potatoes. When she could, she replied, "An angel."

"An angel?" repeated her mother.

"Yes, Mama."

The room quieted. "What did your angel look like, honey," asked Granny Jewel.

"He's not *my* angel, Gwanny! He's the sick lady's angel."

"What did he look like?" asked Papa Tom, gently.

Amy looked at each member of her family. Even Clara, standing in the kitchen doorway, was staring.

"He looked like angels are supposed to look!"

"We want you to tell us, Amy," said her mother.

Amy sighed. She was beginning to lose patience with her family. "He was wearing a white dress that looked like a cloud, and wings as thin as a spider web. He had a shiny face, but not like a light bulb."

"Did he look at you or speak?" asked Granny Jewel. All waited as Amy took another bite of creamed potatoes.

"No, he didn't talk. He kept looking at the sick lady."

A voice from the doorway interrupted. "Praise the Lord!" cried Clara, waving the hem of her apron. "The Lord sent his angel to end that sweet lady's suffering and take her home to be with Him." Clara stepped back into the kitchen, still waving her arms and praising God.

Granny Jewel slipped out of her chair and went into the kitchen. "Clara," she whispered, "we don't know if Amy *really* saw an angel. Try to get a hold of yourself. We don't want to alarm the children."

Clara stopped in mid-sentence, lowered her arms and said, "Those words were out of the mouth of one of God's own babes. The veil was dropped from her eyes for a moment to give us mortals a message of life and hope, even in the midst of death."

"I agree with you, Clara. However . . ."

"However, nothing! You Episcopalians have no idea how to enjoy your religion." Clara picked up her wooden stirring spoon and advanced on the dining room. "Mark my words!" she declared, "That angel's taking Mackie's mama home with him tonight, so you best be dusting off your funeral clothes!"

Chapter 6

By noon the following day, neighbors and friends knew Mrs. Fuller had passed away in the night. All agreed it was for the best, that she had suffered enough.

"She's sleeping in the sweet bosom of Jesus," declared Clara, not surprised when she heard the news. The rest of the day she went about her work wearing the 'I told you so' expression the family had seen many times.

Mackie's Aunt Mabel, due on Friday, came on the four o'clock bus Wednesday. By the time she arrived, the Fuller house had been straightened and food brought in by neighbors and ladies from the Baptist church.

During lunch on Thursday, loud banging was heard on the back door of the Mitchell home. Clara, startled, saw the pitiful figure of Mackie Fuller, his nose flattened against the screen.

"Where's Joshua?" he demanded.

Clara, deciding this was no fit time to stress good manners, replied, "Come in, Mackie. Joshua's eating his lunch. Would you like a sandwich?"

"No, uh, thanks," he stammered, stepping inside the kitchen. He was dressed in dark pants and white shirt. The top button, under stress, caused the points of the collar to turn up. He had neglected to fasten another button farther down, causing his tummy to look as if it were trying to escape, the tail of the shirt crawling over the top of his pants.

Joshua appeared at the kitchen door. "Hello, Mackie." He hesitated only a moment, then blurted, "I'm sorry about your mama."

"Yeah," the older boy replied, looking down. His head jerked up. "Come out on the porch. I gotta tell you something." He held the screen door. "Hurry, I don't got much time."

Outside, the boys sat on the top step. Neither spoke for a moment. Finally, Mackie sighed, "I haven't been able to figure why God wanted my mama up in Heaven. Then, last night it came to me." He paused. Lower lip trembling, he turned and faced Joshua. "Back before I knew you, I had a baby brother. He didn't live very long, so I never got to play with him. Mama rocked him a lot and sang to him so he wouldn't cry." The older boy struggled for words. "I never heard her sing anymore after he died." He seemed to carefully choose his words. "I figure he must be up in Heaven squawling his head off. God took her up there so she could rock him and keep him quiet. She didn't die till now, because God was waiting until I was old enough to take care of myself."

Joshua nodded. "You definitely can take care of yourself, Mackie."

The older boy got up, dusting off the seat of his dark pants. "Are you coming to the funeral?" he asked, starring.

"Yeah, the whole family's coming. Papa Tom is closing the grocery store for the afternoon so everybody can go."

"Wow," whispered Mackie.

Sarah came out on the porch and sat beside her brother. "Let us know if you need anything. We're all here to help you, Mackie."

His expression hardened. "Thanks, but I don't need nothing from nobody. I got these," he pounded a fist in the palm of his hand. "My daddy and me can take care of ourselves." He turned and walked toward the hole in the fence, not looking back.

Sarah joined her brother on the top step. "The tougher he acts, the more I feel sorry for him," she said.

Joshua slipped his hand in his sister's. "What happens in a home where there isn't a mama? Who cooks and cleans and all that stuff?"

"I guess everybody in the family has to pitch in and help. Daddies learn to cook and the kids clean and make up their beds."

"I don't care how clean the house is, it's not the same if there's no mama when you come home from school."

"You're right, little brother. Now, if we don't start getting ready, our mama is going to be looking for us."

Clara and Amy were armed with a tall pitcher of lemonade when the family came home. The women took off their hats, and the men loosened their ties before relaxing with a cool drink. When everyone was seated, Amy proudly handed out napkins, followed by Clara with a tray of glasses. Granny Jewel poured and Sarah handed each a glass. For a few moments, all were quiet, enjoying the cold liquid.

"Joshua," asked Uncle Herb, "isn't Mackie on the Episcopal boys' baseball team? I thought they'd be at the funeral for their teammate."

"No, Uncle Herb. He told me he quit the team after two days."

"Why, isn't he a good player?"

"Oh, he's a great player, but the coach wouldn't let him smoke in the outfield."

"Oh."

Herb Mitchell changed the subject. "Mama, Daddy, Miriam and I are thinking about moving."

"Good Heavens! You're not moving away, are you?"

Patiently, Herb explained. "No, Mama. We're not moving away. We're looking for a house."

Miriam interrupted, "The apartment is too small. Most of our wedding gifts are still packed away because there's no place to put them. It's not too bad when I'm teaching since both of us are away all day, but I have felt cramped this summer."

"Have you seen a house for sale?" asked Papa Tom.

"I've fallen in love with one on Moore Street, but Herb doesn't like it," answered Miriam, returning her empty glass to the tray.

"Moore Street! That's four blocks away!" exclaimed Granny Jewel. "A big house is a lot of work and expense. You'd be better off staying where you are."

Herb turned and faced his mother. "There's no way we can ever start a family where we are now, Mama. You would like a few more grandchildren, wouldn't you?"

"I love a big house. The sooner you get one the better," she replied, refilling each glass.

"The house I like is across the street from your friend, Miss Nettie. She would be a good neighbor. I don't know the people on either side, but I'm sure they're friendly like other people in town."

"Daddy, the house is old and needs a lot of repairs. The owner said it leaks around some of the windows in a rain storm."

"The windows are nine panes over six, Mother Jewel. They give the house a gracious appearance."

"The floors slope, you feel like you're on board a ship in rough seas," argued Herb.

"The floors are narrow oak strips. Sanded and varnished, they would be the most beautiful floors in town," said Miriam, staring at her husband.

"The roof leaks, and the paint is peeling off the cracked walls," said Herb, returning her stare.

"The roof needs new shingles, cracked walls can be repaired, and I'm pretty handy with a paint brush."

"I think it would be more practical to buy a lot, and build a new house. It would have modern conveniences, and wouldn't leak," argued Herb.

"I don't want a shiny new house. I want a gracious old one that has a history. I want one that has protected and sheltered families before us. The one I have fallen in love with has wide, ornate moulding around every window and door, fireplaces, and window seats, just like yours, Mother Jewel," pleaded Miriam.

"Of course we would never try to influence you in such a big decision," spoke Jewel Mitchell, not seeing her husband roll his eyes.

"Supper is served," interrupted Clara, ending the discussion. Papa Tom waited until the room had emptied. "Son," he said, "wait a moment." With lowered voice, "A man has his work, and is away from home all day. His wife turns their house into a home for him and their children. The expression, 'A man's home is his castle,' may be true, but it's the wife who makes it so."

"You're right, Daddy," returned Herb, looking determined. "If Miriam's heart is set on getting that old house, then she'll have it. I'd give her the moon, if she asked for it."

The father patted his son on the back as they entered the dining room.

After the evening meal Papa Tom settled down in his favorite chair to listen to the news. Suddenly, he heard a loud click, followed by a deafening silence. He looked up, not believing anyone would dare touch the radio dial, and saw his wife.

"Jewel," he thundered, "what have you done?"

"The news was the same, last night and again tonight. It's a beautiful evening, and I want to go for a walk," she said, tugging at his sleeve.

"Can't you wait a few more minutes?" he asked as he was dragged across the room. "What's the big rush?"

On the sidewalk, Papa Tom stopped. "I suppose we're going to stroll down Moore Street."

"Of course we're going to stroll down Moore Street," replied his wife.

Papa Tom stopped suddenly, putting his hand on his wife's shoulder. "Honey, promise me right now, you will *not* interfere in the kids' lives. Where they live is strictly their decision."

"Yes, dear, I promise," she said, looking into her husbands deep brown eyes.

"Do we still have to take a walk?" he asked, hurrying to catch up.

"Of course, dear. I want to see my children's house before it gets dark."

Two days later, Herb Mitchell came into the grocery store, waving a thick, blue envelope. He hurried toward the office where his father was working. "Dad," he called, "the fearful deed is done."

Papa Tom looked over glasses sitting on the end of his nose. Lowering his fountain pen he repeated, "Fearful deed? What are you talking about, Herb?"

"The house! Miriam's dream house. It's ours!" He handed the envelope to his father. "Of course the bank has the deed until it is paid for, but it's ours, and the bank's."

"Have you told Miriam?"

Herb sat in a chair and faced his father. "No, I'm going to surprise her."

"When do we get to see inside? Your mother and I walked past last night, but couldn't see much."

"The former owners will be out the first of July. That's when we can start making repairs. I hope we can be in August first, that way Miriam can enjoy decorating before she goes back to school, and I won't have to pay another forty dollars rent at the apartment." Herb carefully placed the packet of papers in the top drawer of the wooden file cabinet and put on a white apron. He grinned at his father. "I can't wait to see her face when she finds out we own her dream house."

The next morning Herb Mitchell arrived at work wearing a serious expression. "Is anything wrong," asked Papa Tom when he saw his son. "You look like you lost your best friend."

Herb came over and started helping his father open cartons of canned goods. "Miriam and I had only seen the house at night after I came home from work. Yesterday we stopped in during my lunch break." Herb looked at his father. "Daddy, the house looks different in bright daylight." He gave a deep sigh and sat down on an unopened carton of string beans. "That house is in terrible shape! It's going to take more money to fix it up than it did to buy it." He looked up. "Even Miriam is discouraged. She came home and cried, saying she had gotten us in this mess, and that she should have listened to me and settled for a new house. I started to agree with her, but instead I told her we'd have it good as new in no time."

"That was very wise, my son," Papa Tom slid another carton of canned string beans over and sat down. "You're right, the fearful deed is done. Now what are you going to do."

"Math Chapman, a fellow I went to school with, is a contractor. He's going to meet me at lunch today to take a look at the house. Maybe he won't find too much wrong."

"I know Math, and he is the best contractor in town. Whatever he says you can count on."

"Is this the conference room?" rang a merry voice. Each looked up to see Sarah standing beside a sack of potatoes, tying an apron around her waist. "It must be serious, judging from the look on your faces."

"Sarah, Miriam's dream home may turn out to be a nightmare home."

"I'll bet it's built better than the houses that have been built since the war. Daddy says pre-fab houses won't hold up many years. Your house may be tired looking, but I bet it'll be here a hundred years from now. It needs some sprucing up and we can all pitch in and help."

Herb looked at his father. "That is one smart girl. Who do you think she takes after?"

"She takes after her grandfather, of course."

Chapter 7

Posters were everywhere advertising a Fourth of July dance at the Pavilion on Atlantic Beach with a band coming all the way from New York. It was to be the highlight of the summer social season. Dates and what to wear were the topic of discussion among women of all ages. Every beauty parlor in Beaufort and Morehead City were booked well in advance. James Bowers was arriving from Raleigh two days before the big event hoping to relax and enjoy Clara's cooking.

On Monday night before the dance on Saturday, Sarah and her grandparents overheard Peggy talking long distance. "We miss you too, darling. Now, listen carefully as I tell you which of my evening clothes to bring."

Sarah listened as her mother, in minute detail, described the dress and accessories she wanted James to bring with him.

"Are you writing this down, honey, because if you're not, I'll have to go to New Bern and buy a brand new dress, with matching jewelry, gloves and shoes."

"I'll bet he's picking up a pad and pencil now," said Papa Tom, grinning.

"Oh, and James," she continued, "don't forget your black dress pants and white dinner jacket. You'll be the handsomest man at the dance."

"Mama," interrupted Sarah, "let me speak to Daddy." Hearing her father's voice for the first time in almost a month made Sarah's eyes sting. Quickly blinking away tears, she said, "I love you, Daddy, and miss you." Sarah paused, smiling. "Yes, sir, Clara knows you'll be here in time for supper."

Hearing their sister's voice, Joshua and Amy begged for the phone. "I want to talk to daddy," demanded Joshua.

"Me too, me too," begged Amy, adding to the confusion.

Holding his little sister off with one hand, he gripped the receiver with the other. "Daddy, Mackie's mama died." After a moment, he spoke again. "Yes, sir, I am being a friend. He tells me stuff he don't tell anybody else, and I listen. I even didn't complain when I had to put on Sunday clothes in the middle of the week." Joshua was silent for a moment. "Don't you worry one bit about us. Papa Tom and I are taking care of things."

Sarah, standing nearby, rolled her eyes. "Oh, brother," she muttered.

"All men will be wearing black pants and white jackets," said Papa Tom, abandoning his newspaper. "Why can't women all wear dresses alike? You could keep the dress until it wore out, then buy another one like it. It would save a lot of confusion."

"Oh, you old fuddy-duddy! Every woman at the dance wants to be the prettiest, and nothing makes you feel that way more than a lovely gown and a pair of dainty dancing shoes," explained Granny Jewel.

"You'll be the most beautiful girl at the dance, honey," said Papa Tom, giving his wife a broad grin.

"Why, Thomas Mitchell, are you asking me for a date?"

"Of course. I wouldn't want to deny people an opportunity to see the most gorgeous woman in three counties."

"Oh, Tom, you don't mean that!"

Sarah watched with interest as color appeared in her grandmother's cheeks, making her more beautiful. "If that's the case, then we can double date," said their daughter, stepping into the living room.

"We claim the back seat so I can snuggle with your mother," added Papa Tom.

"There'll be no snuggling *before* the dance. I'm not going to step in the Pavilion with my make-up disturbed."

"Now that's a fine way to talk to the man of your dreams, *and* the man who has ordered an orchid corsage from Beaufort Florist." Papa Tom placed his hands over his heart, as if it were about to break.

She stood and blew her husband a kiss. "Peggy, Sarah, come upstairs and let's see if we can find anything in the wardrobe that will be fit to wear."

"Oh," groaned Papa Tom, "I feel a financial crisis coming!" His words were unheard as the three rapidly climbed the stairs.

When they reached the grandparents' bedroom, Sarah said, "Bruce is coming by tonight. Do you think he'll ask me?"

"It's not too late. You still have several days before the dance," said Granny Jewel.

"Mama, it is OK if I go, isn't it? Of course, I don't have a thing to wear."

"If Bruce invites you, we'll see that you have a proper gown," promised Peggy.

Jewel Mitchell carefully checked dresses in the tall cedar wardrobe, dismissing each. One had already been worn several times, one outdated by its style and another she had never liked. "I think it's the color," she said, tapping a long fingernail against her chin.

"However, there may be one more that's just right. Last spring, the Beaufort Garden Club sponsored a dance at the USO building in Morehead City. I bought a gown for the occasion, but we didn't go. We had terrible spring colds and didn't want to infect anyone." Once more she reached inside, producing a dress covered in white tissue paper. "This may be just the ticket," she announced. Tissue covering gone, the women stared. The last remnants of the day's light shone on the dress, causing it to shimmer and glow.

"Oh, my, Granny Jewel. That is the most beautiful material I have ever seen," exclaimed Sarah. The dress was a soft spring green, with tiny sprigs of white flowers. It had a low neck, dropped waistline and full skirt.

"Mama, you'll be the belle of the ball in that gown," whispered Peggy. "Hold it up against you and let me see how it's going to look."

Jewel Mitchell carefully held the bodice against her, letting the skirt billow around her legs. "That color suits you, Mama. Daddy was right when he said you would be the prettiest woman at the dance." It was obvious a tinge of envy colored the daughter's remarks.

Granny Jewel looked doubtful. "Are you sure it isn't too youthful? It doesn't look like an old lady's dress at all."

"Nonsense, Granny Jewel. You don't look like an old lady. The dress will be perfect." They were interrupted by a knock on the front door. Sarah recognized Bruce's voice. Hurriedly, she grabbed a comb and smoothed her hair.

"Don't rush, sweetheart," instructed her grandmother. "Let him wait a moment. Then descend the stairs as if you were the queen mother."

"Thanks, Granny Jewel," Sarah replied, ignoring her grandmother's detailed instructions.

"Ah, here she is, Bruce," announced Papa Tom. Not wanting to give up his chair in the living room, and knowing the young couple wanted privacy, he suggested, "It's usually cool on the porch in the evening. Don't you all want to sit out there?"

"Thanks, Mr. Mitchell. That sounds like a great idea," replied Bruce, sounding relieved.

Bruce followed as Sarah led the way, each choosing a rocking chair. Bruce immediately dragged his up one inch from Sarah's. "How was your day?" asked Sarah, wondering how she might steer the conversation around to the dance.

"It was nothing special. Pushing a lawn mower is hot, hard work." He looked at Sarah and smiled. "I thought about you all day. Did you think about me?"

Sarah returned his smile, remembering how she had thought of little else than an invitation to the dance. "We were so busy at the store. Several trucks came in and had to be unloaded. Fresh produce has to be gotten in the bins immediately, and invoices checked. Some of the customers were buying groceries for a week and several shrimp boats had to be grubbed up. We got our first Bogue Sound watermelons. They were gone before noon because they are the best."

Bruce agreed. "There's nothing tastes quite like a Bogue Sound melon."

"Papa Tom had promised Joshua a fishing trip, so we were a little short handed." Again Sarah flashed Bruce her finest smile. "I hope things will slow down by the weekend, don't you? I'd hate to have to work on Saturday, especially *this* Saturday." Sarah waited patiently for Bruce to ask her what is special about this weekend. When he didn't respond, she continued. "My father is coming to spend the Fourth of July weekend. He's coming for the big dance at the Pavilion on Atlantic Beach." She stared hopefully at the boy beside her.

"Oh, that's great! I'll get to meet your dad."

Sarah pressed on "You won't see him Saturday night. He and Mama are going to the dance. Actually, my grandparents are going, too." Sarah leaned over and touched the boy's hand. "It's going to be the biggest social event of the season, my grandmother said."

"Hey, Sarah, I just had a great idea!"

"What, Bruce?" she asked, matching his enthusiasm.

"We could babysit for the evening. We'll take your brother and sister for a walk along the waterfront and buy them an ice cream cone at the drug store. When they get tired, we can bring them home, put them to bed and have the evening to ourselves." Bruce waited for Sarah's reaction.

It would sound great if we were seventy years old, she thought. Sarah sank back in her chair. "I never would have thought of that," she mumbled.

When Bruce left, Sarah dragged herself into the house, "Mama," she called.

Peggy's face appeared at the head of the stairs, holding a finger to her lips.

"Mama," she whispered fiercely, "I need to talk to you!"

The mother beckoned, Sarah quickly mounting the steps. At the top, Peggy took her daughter's hand and together they went into Joshua's bedroom, softly closed the door, and sat on the bed that had been Sarah's in summer's past.

"What's the matter, honey?" asked Peggy, still holding her daughter's hand.

"Mama," she wailed softly, "Bruce still hasn't asked me to the dance. Are you *sure* I can't ask him? It isn't fair that a girl has to wait to be asked."

Sarah felt a pat on her shoulder. "That's just the way it is, honey. A young lady of good reputation would *never* ask a boy to take her to the dance."

Sarah stared at the floor. "He wants us to babysit while you all go to the dance. I love my brother and sister, but I don't love the thoughts of spending Saturday night with them."

"You mentioned the dance tonight. He'll think about it, and by tomorrow night, he'll ask you."

Sarah turned to her mother. "I won't have time to find a dress if he doesn't ask tomorrow."

"If he comes by tomorrow night and invites you, I'll call your daddy and have him bring your evening dress you wore at the Honors Banquet in the spring."

Sarah squeezed her mother's hand. "Thanks, Mama. I knew you would know what to do."

The following day, Sarah rushed to answer the phone every time it rang. "Mitchell's Grocery," she answered brightly, hoping each time it would be Bruce. *Maybe he will call because he's so anxious to ask me to the dance,* she hoped. At five o'clock when he still hadn't called, Sarah put her apron in the laundry basket and started home. *He has to ask me tonight,* she decided, *or it will be too late for daddy to bring my dress.* She walked swiftly past a yard where two children were squealing with delight as they played with a garden hose. She envied them their worry-free life.

Dinner was fried fish and cornbread, potato salad and green beans. Sarah knew she would have to suffer through her brother's bragging. He and Papa Tom had caught a bucket full of bluefish trolling in the inlet that morning. She knew it would take several days for him to tire of telling each detail of their trip and she was in no mood to listen to his exaggerated tales.

Before plates were filled, Sarah turned to her grandfather. "Papa Tom," she asked, sounding cross, "why can't a girl ask a boy for a date?"

Papa Tom, holding a large bowl of potato salad, stopped. "Hmmm, let me think." He continued serving himself a large helping, and passed the bowl to Granny Jewel, then turned and looked at his older granddaughter. "I never thought about it. I guess it's the custom, honey. Boys like to do the asking because it makes them feel they are in charge."

Sarah buttered a slice of cornbread. "Well, I don't see what harm it would be for me to ask Bruce to ask me to the dance."

"Oh, honey, you can't do that!" interrupted Granny Jewel, shaking her head. "You would get the reputation of being *forward*."

"Am I being forward just because I want to go to the dance?"

Joshua, busy picking tiny bones from his fish, asked, "I don't understand. If you don't want Sarah to be forward, do you want her to be backward? There's a boy in my class everybody says is backward, and they act like it is something terrible. Should I tell people my sister is backward?"

Sarah turned to her brother and hissed, "If I don't understand, I'm sure you don't, so just keep quiet!"

The silence in the room was followed by their mother's voice. "We're not going to have talk like that at the table. You're not too old to be sent to your room."

"I'll save you the trouble, Mama." Sarah slammed her napkin on the table and got up.

"Sarah, wait," called her grandmother. It was too late. The door to Sarah's bedroom slammed shut.

Joshua's voice broke the silence. "What happened, Mama?" his eyes wide. "Why is Sarah so mad?"

Peggy looked at her son. "She isn't mad, exactly. She's . . . upset, or frustrated, or . . ."

"Or about the business of growing up," interrupted her grandfather. "It's especially hard when you're a teenager."

"Someday I'll be a teenager, and I promise not to act like that."

"Me, too, me, too," echoed Amy.

"Can we get that in writing?" asked their grandfather.

Sarah lay curled in the middle of her bed, feeling more miserable by the minute. *I hate it when I lose my temper, but only someone with a pesky little brother knows how aggravating they can be.* Sarah let out a long sigh. *He was only asking a question.* Her thoughts were interrupted by a light tap on the door. "Come in," she called, sitting up.

One of Clara's mahogany brown hands reached around the door. "Is it safe to come in, or will I get my face eaten off?"

Sarah giggled. "It's safe, Clara, you can come in without worrying." Sarah slid over and made room for the older woman.

Clara lowered herself on the bed, causing metal springs to squeak. She patted Sarah on the knee. "You're right, honey-child. It ain't fair for the boys to have all the say-so. I hope by the time your daughters are your age, things are different. It shouldn't be the end of a girl's reputation for her to call a boy on the phone if she wants to talk to him, and if she wants to go to a dance, she should be able to ask her beau to take her."

"That sounds great, Clara, but how is it going to help me get an invitation for Saturday night?"

"I know a surefire way," the older woman said, looking to be sure no one was listening at the door. Sarah's eyes were riveted on the woman she adored. "Honey," she said softly, "you gotta' use feminine wiles."

Sarah never blinked. "Who are they, Clara?" she whispered.

"Not who, honey, *what*."

"Tell me," urged Sarah, placing her hand over Clara's.

"Well girl, you won't find none of what I tell you written in one of those etiquette books. This is something most women are born knowing."

"How does it work?"

Clara sat straight and sniffed loudly. "To start with, menfolks think they are smarter than us women. They make all the decisions and like to tell us what to do. I'm already seeing signs of it in that little brother of yours."

Sarah, wearing a wry expression, nodded agreement.

"So, what do I have to do?"

"In order to get what *you* want, you have to make them think it's their idea."

Sarah grinned. "How do I do that?"

Clara turned her full attention on the young girl. "Tonight when that boy comes over, you gotta' talk about dancing. Tell him how much you enjoy watching people dancing in the movies. Tell him you're so glad to be sixteen, cause now you're old enough to go out dancing. After awhile, the fog will lift in his brain and he'll invite you to the dance, thinking he's very clever. You're supposed to act surprised and pleased. Before he can change his mind, you accept. 'Why, yes, Bruce, I'd love to go to the dance with you. Thank you for asking.'"

Sarah smiled slowly. "I'll try, Clara."

"Nobody's perfect the first time they do something. You can practice on this boy, and by the time you're marrying age, you'll have it down pat. Take that fancy cousin of yours from Greenville. That girl was born knowing how to get her way." Clara started toward the door. "Now come out here and make peace with your family. I put your supper on the stove so it would stay warm. You've got to keep your strength up if you're going to use feminine wiles."

Sarah, looking troubled, asked, "Clara, have women been doing this very long?"

"Honey, women been doing this since Eve was in the garden."

Clara opened the door to leave. "Wait, please," begged Sarah. "How about Mama and Granny Jewel? I know they've never done this before."

Clara leaned on the door, one hand on her hip. "I don't know about your mama, but if there was a contest today, your grandmother would be crowned 'Queen of Feminine Wiles.'"

Chapter 8

Sarah was sitting on the front porch holding Spooky in her lap Wednesday evening when Bruce arrived. He chose the chair closest to Sarah and leaned over to pet Spooky. The cat quickly abandoned Sarah and jumped in Bruce's lap.

"Good evening, Spooky," he said, scratching her under the chin. He was rewarded with her soft rumbling purr. He looked at Sarah and smiled. "I love the story of how you found Spooky under the Methodist church." His tone grew more serious and he reached over to take her hand. "Sarah, you are so special. I don't know another girl who would do such a scary thing to rescue a kitten."

Sarah smiled. "That's silly, Bruce. I'm like other girls. I like pretty clothes, romantic movies and dancing. I especially like dancing."

"Hmmm," Bruce murmured. "That's nice." He turned suddenly, scaring Spooky, who jumped down to chase a cricket. "Let's walk downtown and get a Coca-Cola. There's something I want to ask you."

Sarah felt her heart do a flip when she glanced at her friend's brown eyes and wide grin. "Sure, Bruce. I'll tell Mama we're going to get a cold drink."

Sarah hurried into the house and found her mother folding clothes on the dining room table. "Mama," she whispered excitedly, "we may have to call Daddy tonight. I think Bruce is finally going to ask me to go to the dance."

Peggy smiled over a mountain of sweet smelling clothes. "Oh, that's wonderful. Should we call your daddy now?"

Sarah glanced toward the front porch, and then looked at her mother. "We're going to walk downtown," she whispered. "Maybe we'd better wait until I get back."

"Good thinking and good luck."

As Sarah walked slowly toward the porch, she chanted, "I am kin to Marnie and I want to go to the dance. I know about feminine wiles and I intend to use them." Her jaw was set, her lips a thin line.

As they walked toward the waterfront, Sarah slipped her hand in Bruce's and was rewarded with a squeeze. Bell's Drug Store was almost empty when they stopped in for a cool drink. The druggist was in the back of the store and one bored clerk was standing near the cash register. Sarah noticed that Bruce seemed restless. He drew designs in the condensation that formed on the glass top table. "Let's take our drinks and walk down to the Inlet Inn dock. It's more private." The disinterested clerk rewarded them with a huge yawn as they left.

The couple walked slowly along the waterfront, listening to the gentle waves lapping against the break wall. After sitting on the end of the dock for several minutes, Sarah remembered Clara's instructions. "Oh, look, Bruce, the stars are out tonight. They look like they're dancing, don't they?"

"The reason they look like they're moving and twinkling is because of our atmosphere and because they are so far away." He moved closer and put his arm around the pretty girl beside him. With the other arm he pointed out constellations.

Oh, brother, thought Sarah, pretending interest. I'll have to try again. While Bruce was giving a lecture on the position of heavenly bodies, Sarah interrupted.

"Bruce, look at the light from the moon reflected on the water. It makes the waves look like they're dancing. I would love to be dancing on the waves, wouldn't you?"

"Wave action is determined by the wind," Bruce patiently explained. He turned toward Sarah and paused a moment, moving closer. "I do see the moon's reflection dancing in your eyes." He bent his head and touched his lips to hers. When he moved away, he murmured, "That kiss made my heart dance, Sarah."

Sarah straightened. "How about your feet, Bruce? Did our kiss make your feet feel like dancing." Sarah knew she was talking too loud, destroying the tender moment. "Do you feel like dancing enough to ask me to the dance on Saturday night?" Sarah threw caution to the wind, knowing she had failed her first exercise in using 'feminine wiles."

Bruce moved away, shock written on his face. "I'm sorry, Sarah. I don't dance and wouldn't know how."

"That's OK, Bruce," she enthused. "I can teach you. Nancy and I taught Uncle Herb when he and Aunt Miriam were courting."

Bruce sighed and slowly shook his head. "It's not that. My family believes dancing is sinful. Nobody in my church dances. I'm so sorry," he added softly.

Sarah took off her sandals and dipped her feet in the cool salt water. "It's alright. I don't have to go to the dance."

"We have plans for Saturday night, remember? We're going to keep the kids," he reminded her.

Sarah thought about the bright lights, a band from New York, ladies in lovely dresses on the arms of men looking like Clark Gable.

So much for feminine wiles, she thought. "Bruce," she said suddenly, "what did you want to ask me?"

Bruce sighed deeply and stared across the channel. The only sound was the cry of a black skimmer gliding along the edge of the shore, looking for supper. "Sarah," he said finally, "will you be my steady girl?"

Sarah was silent. Steady girl? Lots of her friends were going steady. This would be something exciting to write and tell her friends in Raleigh. Nancy would be home soon and would be so surprised. "Yes, Bruce. I'd love to be your steady girl."

Bruce reached in his shirt pocket and handed her a small box wrapped in white tissue. "This is for you, Sarah." She quickly opened it and saw a rhinestone heart on a silver chain.

"Oh, Bruce it's lovely!" she exclaimed, knowing he had mowed lawns in the summer heat to afford a necklace from Bell's Jewelers. "I'll wear it every day," Sarah promised and they walked slowly toward home. "Look at the way the light danc . . . I mean, look at the way the light makes the rhinestones sparkle!"

Sarah didn't invite her steady beau in that night, but told him goodnight on her front steps. Bruce held her hand tightly. "I'm sorry about the dance, Sarah, but that's just the way it is."

"I understand, Bruce," she said, trying to keep disappointment out of her voice. They kissed goodnight, Sarah enjoying the warm feeling of his lips on hers.

Once inside, Sarah tiptoed upstairs. "Mama." She whispered, "Where are you?" Neither her mother nor sister were in the bedroom.

"Sarah," called her mother as she stepped into the hall. "We're on the upstairs porch."

Sarah hurried out. There was a cool breeze stirring the tops of the trees. "Amy couldn't get to sleep inside because the house is still like an oven."

The three year old was curled in her mother's lap, sleeping soundly. Street light cast a faint glow on the mother and child. "I'll put her down in a few minutes and we can call your father," said Peggy, smiling at her older daughter.

"There's no need, Mama. Bruce isn't going to take me to the dance. Neither he nor his family believe in dancing."

Sarah's news was met with silence. "Oh, Honey," Peggy finally said, "I'm so sorry. Try not to be too disappointed. You're young and there are plenty more dances in your future."

"I know, Mama, but it won't be this one. I've waited sixteen years to go to a real dance with a band and ladies in evening dresses."

Sarah's announcement that she would not be going to the dance was a disappointment to the family. "You should have set your cap for a nice Episcopal boy. Episcopalians enjoy dancing," declared Granny Jewel.

"But I really like Bruce, and I understand how he feels."

At four o'clock the front door flew open and James Bowers announced his arrival. "Where is my family?" his voice boomed. From all areas of the house he was rushed by loved ones. After greetings and hugs, he declared, "I'm going to need some help unloading the car. There are more fancy dresses, lacy underskirts and sparkly shoes than I know what to do with." Peggy Bowers rushed to get her formal clothes and hurry them upstairs to the bedroom so it would not remind Sarah of the dance.

"My beautiful niece looks like she lost her best friend," declared Uncle Herb the next morning. "Where is that smile that makes boys' hearts skip a beat?"

"Unless you can produce a handsome young prince who will ask me to the ball, there's nothing to smile about. Actually, Uncle Herb, I still couldn't go, because I told Bruce I'd be his steady girl." Sarah reached for the rhinestone heart she wore around her neck. Her fingers closed around the cool stone.

"Going steady, are you? That sounds serious to me. I hope you're not planning on getting married any time soon."

"No, Uncle Herb. I don't think I'll ever get married. Boys are too much work." Sarah busily dusted the same shelf of canned string beans three times. "Say, are you and Miriam going to the dance?"

Herb Mitchell placed a yellow pencil behind one ear and folded his arms. "We talked about it, but Miriam is so wrapped up in fixing the house, we decided not to go."

Sarah straightened bags of corn meal and flour. "Things are very uncomfortable at our house. Nobody talks about the dance because I can't go. It makes me feel bad because they look sad." Sarah looked at her uncle. "You know what I mean?"

"Uh, I think I do."

Sarah moved away to wait on a customer. When the bell on the door tinkled, Uncle Herb walked over to the cash register. "I have an idea, Sarah. Why don't you come over to the house tonight and help Miriam and me. I promise we'll talk about paint and window putty, termites and leaky roofs. I'll call Miriam and tell her to make some extra sandwiches and you can eat with us. There's no furniture, so we'll spread a picnic supper on the floor. You won't have to go home until bedtime."

"Thanks, Uncle Herb. That sounds like a great idea," said Sarah gratefully. "I'll call Mama and tell her not to expect me for dinner. I'll be dining elsewhere." Uncle Herb went back to his work, happy he had finally coaxed a smile from his niece.

Sarah was surprised to see how many improvements had already been made to the gracious old house. The smell of new lumber filled the rooms. It was hard to walk with tools, saw horses and boards piled everywhere. In the upstairs hall a commode sat, looking out of place.

"Is this a new decorating idea?" Sarah teased. "It won't look out of place if you put a flower arrangement inside."

"Welcome, Sarah," called Miriam from one of the bedrooms. "The picnic is spread and ice cream is melting. The radio said possible showers this evening." Herb Mitchell appeared in the doorway. "We need to eat before it rains, or we'll be the first picnickers ever to get leaked on."

"Never mind, dear," laughed Miriam. "I brought umbrellas." For the next thirty minutes Sarah laughed at the silly antics of her aunt and uncle, knowing they were making every effort to cheer her.

At ten o'clock Herb Mitchell called a halt to the painting. Brushes were placed in containers of turpentine so they could be used again. While they were scrubbing paint off their hands and elbows, Sarah asked, "What color are you going to paint the little room next to yours?"

"Well, Sarah, we're going to give it a coat of white after the cracks in the plaster are patched. We're not sure of a color yet." Her uncle gave Miriam a special smile.

"You see, Honey," explained Miriam, giving Sarah a hug. "We're hoping someday that room will be a nursery."

"Oh," breathed Sarah. "At last I'll be cousin Sarah. I can come summers and babysit, so you can go to parties and dances." When she said dances, her smile faded.

"Now don't you despair, my girl," said Uncle Herb. "Someday our baby will be a teenager, and babysit for your children so you and your husband can go out for the evening. Life is like a wheel, family members fitting together like cogs, making the wheel turn."

Miriam and Sarah waited on the porch while Herb closed the house. They walked the few blocks home by the light from street lamps on every corner. The couple walked Sarah to the front door of her grandparents' home. "Thank you for a fun evening," said Sarah. "It helped a lot."

"Thanks for your help, too," added Uncle Herb. "You're good with a paint brush."

Sarah tiptoed in, hooking the screen door. A lamp on the hall table lit her way through the house. In the dining room the ironing board was up. Dresses, pressed and ready, hung from door facings, ready for the dance. Even in the half light, her grandmother's gown glowed and shimmered.

Sarah awoke on Saturday morning to the sound of Clara's voice. She dressed quickly in a clean pair of shorts and a shirt and stepped in the kitchen. "Clara, what's wrong?" she asked, alarmed.

"It's this tom-foolery mess draped all over the dining room. How am I supposed to put a decent meal on the table?"

Sarah took the dresses and lace petticoats hanging from the door facings and carried them upstairs. With every step she heard the soft rustle of the fabric, whispering the promise of an exciting evening. Oh, well, she thought, I'll go to a dance when Uncle Herb, who doesn't have a child, can babysit for my baby that I won't have for at least eight more years. Hmmm, I hope I won't be too old to 'cut a rug.'

Breakfast was disorganized. Joshua appeared first, dragging Amy. "My parents are still in bed," he reported. "Amy and I are about to starve so we came downstairs to find Clara. He helped Amy climb into the high chair which no longer needed a tray.

Clara appeared with two plates of crispy bacon and soft, fluffy scrambled eggs. "Just look at my poor babies left to fend for themselves." She showed her displeasure by bringing the heavy plates down with a smack on the dining room table.

While the children were eating, the grandparents appeared. Granny Jewel was clearly in charge. "Now Thomas, this morning you must go to Ideal Dry Cleaners and get your dinner jacket. Don't wait until this afternoon."

Papa Tom was unrolling the morning paper, his eyes searching the day's headlines. "Yes, dear, yes, dear," he nodded indifferently. It was obvious to Sarah, who was helping serve food, that her grandfather was paying very little attention to his wife's instructions.

"I do wish Peggy would get up," she continued. "We have to be at the beauty parlor by one o'clock." She noticed Sarah taking her place at the table. "How was your evening, dear? Do you think the house will be finished by the end of the month?"

Before Sarah could answer, Clara brought in a tray of hot toast. "This family needs to get organized," she announced. "Clara ain't no short order cook. Do you see me wearing a fancy white uniform with my name stitched on the pocket? Do I have a pad and pencil in my hand ready to say, 'May I take your order, please?'"

"Oh, Clara, please forgive us. It's just that there's so much going on today. Tom needs to go to the store this morning. James is taking the children to the beach for a swim, and Peggy and I have to . . . ." Jewel Mitchell's voice grew fainter when she glanced at her older granddaughter.

"It's gonna' have to be all right this time, just so you don't make a habit of it." Clara gave a loud sniff. "I'm going in the kitchen now and cook up some of Mr. James's favorite sausage, eggs and cheese." No one noticed that Granny Jewel's eyes had narrowed, and she was tapping her chin with one tapered finger.

An hour later, when the wringer washing machine had finished its cycle, Granny Jewel walked into the kitchen and put her arm around

Clara's shoulder. "We really are making extra work for you, Clara. I want you to know how much we appreciate all you do."

Clara, her kitchen in order once more, smiled. "You all are family as much as William and the boys. I may huff and puff a lot, but I don't really mind a little extra work."

"I'm going to hang out the clothes. That will help a little." Before Clara could protest, Granny Jewel stepped out of the back door and into the utility room. Minutes later, Clara heard a loud cry. Flying to the back door, she was horrified to see the grandmother on the ground at the foot of the steps, wet clothes spilled from the laundry basket.

Clara burst through the door. "Jesus, lover of my soul, what has happened?" she cried, hurrying down the steps and kneeling beside Granny Jewel. "Are you killed? Is your neck broke? Speak to me!" She tried to pull Granny Jewel into a sitting position.

"Oh, Clara, I turned my ankle. I think it might be broken. One minute I was coming down the steps with the laundry basket and the next, I was on the ground. My ankle hurts so badly I can hardly draw breath."

"I got to get you in the house, but you weigh too much for me to carry." Even in the fog of pain, Jewel Mitchell cut her eye at her life-long friend. "Now, I didn't say you weigh too much," Clara assured the lady on the ground, wiping dirt and grass stains from her grandmother's clothes, "so don't be giving me that squinty-eyed look."

Clara rushed into the house and grabbed the hall telephone. She dialed the number of Mitchell's Grocery and waited impatiently until someone answered. "Tom Mitchell, you best be getting on home. Jewel has fallen down the back steps and can't get up!"

Minutes later, Herb Mitchell, followed by his father, burst through the front door and raced through the house. Peggy and Sarah had joined Clara and sat on either side of the injured woman.

"Sarah," barked Papa Tom, "go upstairs and turn the covers down on our bed. Find extra pillows so we can elevate her leg."

Slowly, with help, Jewel Mitchell was able to get to her feet, putting all her weight on one foot. With her arm around her son and husband, she managed the back steps. Finally, Herb swept his mother up in his arms. "Somebody open the door. I can carry mama."

When they got upstairs, Sarah had the bed ready. Herb placed his mother gently on the soft bed with several soft white pillows at her back. More pillows were placed under the injured ankle.

"I'm calling Dr. Maxwell, right now," declared Papa Tom.

"No!" exclaimed Granny Jewel. "I will be fine. I'm sure it's not broken. By tomorrow I'll be good as new. Now, everyone go about your business. I just need to rest."

"I'm going to make you a cup of hot tea," said Clara.

"I'll get you an aspirin," added Peggy.

"I'll make a cold pack to put on your ankle," added Papa Tom, hurrying downstairs. Before he reached the kitchen he heard muffled sobs. Stepping in the room, he realized it was Clara, catching her tears with the hem of her apron.

"Clara, what's the matter?" he asked softly.

Clara lowered her apron, tears flowing freely. "It was all my fault, Tom Mitchell. That should have been me toting that heavy laundry basket. She grabbed the wash before I could dry my hands, and sailed off the porch." Clara dabbed at her tear-stained face.

Papa Tom put his arm around Clara's shoulder. Patting gently he said in a soothing voice, "It could have happened to anybody. It certainly wasn't your fault. I'm sure in a few days she'll be as spry as ever." He struggled to get ice cubes from a tray. "Clara, I know you'd be crying a lot louder if it was me up there in bed."

Clara's tears stopped suddenly. "Oh, there wouldn't be time for tears if it was you. We'd all be waiting on you day and night, hand and foot. 'Get me this, get me that.'"

Papa Tom rolled ice cubes in a dish towel and hurried upstairs, content to see that Clara's tears had dried.

James and the two younger children met him in the hall. Before Papa Tom could tell all that had happened, Joshua, followed by Amy, rushed upstairs. It was the first time either of them had seen their grandmother in bed past dawn's light.

"Granny Jewel," wailed Joshua, "you're not going to be crippled, are you?" Suddenly, he brightened. "Are you going to get a wooden leg like Ramie?"

Amy climbed in bed, wearing her salty bathing suit and a fine coating of beach sand. She patted her grandmother's arm. "Can I kiss your boo-boo and make it well?"

With all the family in attendance, Granny Jewel made an announcement. "Thank you everyone. It's wonderful to feel so loved. "Now," she paused and looked at the concerned faces. "I want to talk to Sarah and Tom. Everyone else go down for lunch."

The family exchanged quick glances, but did as the grandmother requested. When only two were left, Granny Jewel beckoned for Sarah to come near. "Come sit by me and listen carefully." She took Sarah's hand in hers. "Honey, there's no way I'll be able to go to the dance. Your grandfather has been looking forward to tonight for weeks." Papa Tom opened his mouth to protest but quickly closed it when he saw his wife's eyes resting on him.

"My dress and slippers should fit perfectly. You will take my appointment at the beauty parlor and when you get home, we'll try on the dress and see if it needs any alterations."

Sarah tried to protest, but was stopped by her grandmother's hand. "If you want to make me happy, you'll do as I say."

"Yes, Ma'am," said Sarah, trying not to show her excitement. "I promise to come up and sit on your bed tomorrow and tell you everything that happened."

"Now, everyone out, and let me rest."

When lunch was over, the house became silent. All had gone on errands or were occupied downstairs. Jewel Mitchell spotted a new Life magazine on a table across the room. Without thinking, she tiptoed across the room, grabbed the magazine and turned to hurry back to bed. Horrified, she saw Clara standing in the doorway, a lunch tray in her hands. For an awful moment, neither spoke.

"Um-hum, I see what you're up to, deceiving the people you love most. I never thought you'd do such a thing. Your family's all upset over your accident, and you're up here flitting around the room like a jack rabbit."

"Are you going to tell," Granny Jewel asked fearfully.

A voice at the foot of the stairs interrupted Clara. "Is Mama all right? Should we cancel our appointments?"

Clara, eyes on her employer and lifelong friend, replied. "No, honey. You run along and I'll tend to your mama." Clara whispered loudly, "Your secret is safe with me. Now get back in this bed and don't make me a bigger liar than I already am."

"I'll always be grateful to you, Clara."

"I know that," said Clara, straightening bed covers and plumping pillows. She walked to the door and turned. "There's only one more thing I'm going to say. You should be out there in Hollywood. You can out act Bette Davis any day."

Chapter 9

"Hurry, Mama, or we'll be late," called Sarah, standing at the foot of the stairs.

"I'm coming, honey. Let me check on mama." Sarah could hear her grandmother's raised voice.

"I'm perfectly fine, Peggy, honey. Sarah's right. If you don't hurry, you'll miss your appointment, and not even president Truman could get you another one this late."

Peggy Bowers hurried down, grabbing her purse and daughter. They burst through the screen door, letting it slam behind them.

"I'm excited about tonight, Sarah. I'm sorry Mama can't go, but it will be so much fun with you and Daddy."

"Bruce called. Since we're going steady, I asked him if he would be upset if I had a date with my grandfather."

"What did he say?" laughed Peggy, enjoying her older daughter's introduction to the world of boys and dating. They appeared to be sisters laughing and giggling as they hurried to the beauty parlor.

"Bruce said as long as my date was over sixty-five, it would be fine."

"Going steady is a serious commitment, Sarah. You won't be able to date anyone else." Peggy sighed. "Sixteen is such a carefree time.

You're old enough to make your own decisions, yet young enough to not have adult worries and responsibilities. You should be dating a lot of different boys at your age."

"I know, Mama," said Sarah hurrying to keep up with her mother. "It seems if you are seen with one boy, others won't ask you out, so you might as well be going steady."

The first person Sarah saw in the beauty parlor was Emily. "Hello, Sarah," she said. "Are you ready to get glamorous?"

"I didn't know you were scheduled to do my grandmother's hair."

Emily gave the girl a broad wink. "I wasn't, honey, but I pulled a switch-a-roo when I heard you were coming in her place."

Sarah sat in Emily's chair and faced the large mirror. The hairdresser put one hand on the back of the chair, the other on her hip. "What'll it be today? If you're going to the big dance, we can't have you looking like a school girl. This is a high powered social event. Let's see what we can do to make you look sophisticated." Emily buried her fingers in Sarah's thick, brown hair. "What I wouldn't give to have healthy hair like yours!"

"What's the difference?"

"Oh, honey, all the years I bleached my hair didn't help. Maybe now it will be better since this is my natural color." Emily absently patted her curls.

"How are your wedding plans coming along?" asked Sarah, changing the subject.

Emily smiled. "It's not going to be a big wedding. We'd rather spend our money on necessities, like rent. Did you know we've rented your aunt and uncle's apartment? It will be ours August first."

August first, thought Sarah. *Oh, brother, there's a lot to be done before they can move in that leaky old house!*

Sarah's thoughts were interrupted. "Describe your dress, and then we can decide what to do with your hair."

Emily listened carefully as Sarah explained. "I have a long dress, but it's in Raleigh, so I'm wearing my grandmother's. It's light green, and made of rayon so it's soft and clingy. The skirt is full at the bottom, and should be good for dancing."

"Is this your first big dance?" asked Emily, pouring shampoo on Sarah's hair.

"Yes, but my family rolls back the rug sometimes and we practice the latest steps in the living room. You should see my parents. They act like they're on their honeymoon, daddy steals kisses, and Mama pretends to be shocked. Papa Tom likes to clown around, and leaves Granny Jewel standing in the middle of the floor with hands on her hips while he dances around her. He declares she can't keep up with him, and she says she's not going to make a fool of herself." Sarah paused, while Emily caught her wet hair in a towel. "I'm sorry she can't go tonight, but I'm sure glad I can go in her place!"

"A soft, clingy dress needs a sophisticated hair-do. I think we need to put your hair up."

"Yes," agreed Sarah, "I was hoping you would say that."

"I want to see my beautiful girls," were the first words Sarah and her mother heard when they stepped in the front door. Both hurried up, bursting into the grandmother's bedroom. They were speechless for a moment. Granny Jewel lay back on a bank of snow white pillows embroidered with pastel flowers, trimmed with wide, Irish lace. Her hair, perfectly combed, lay in gentle waves around her face. She was wearing a pink gown and matching robe trimmed in pastel lace. Lipstick, rouge and an aura of delicate cologne surrounded the woman, her injured foot resting on a stack of soft pillows.

"Why, Mama, I declare you look like the queen of Sheba. If I ever sustain a serious injury, I hope I look as glamorous as you."

Heads turned as Clara, tray in hand, stepped into the room. "Now, don't you two be aggravating this poor woman. Can't you see she's suffering? You skedaddle so she can get some rest."

"Oh, no, Clara," Granny Jewel said quickly. "I'm feeling much better." She hastened to add, "Sarah should try on the dress. It may need to be altered."

"Oh, yes," agreed Sarah. "I want to try on the dress."

Before she looked in the mirror, Sarah could tell the dress was going to be very different from any dress she had ever worn. The fabric was so delicate, it was almost like wearing a petticoat. After Peggy zipped the dress, Sarah stepped in front of the mirror. The dress, molding itself to every curve, made Sarah appear much older than her sixteen years. The sophisticated hairstyle also added years to Sarah's age.

"Oh, yes," breathed Granny Jewel. "That's exactly the effect I was hoping for."

"Mama, that dress is much too old for Sarah. She needs something with ruffles and bows."

"Bows, ah, yes! Clara, please take my nail scissors and clip that floppy bow tacked on the shoulder." When the bow had been tossed aside, the dress had no adornment.

"It looks awfully plain," whined Peggy.

"Honey," said Granny Jewel from her throne, "Sarah's youth and beauty is all the adornment she needs."

"When I was sixteen, you never would have allowed me out of the house in a dress like that."

"You forget, Peggy," answered the grandmother, "her escort is her grandfather, accompanied by her parents. I think she'll be safe. Now, Sarah, look in the closet and bring the shoe box on the left."

Sarah placed the box on the bed beside her grandmother. Carefully, Granny Jewel opened the box, and folded aside white tissue paper. A pair of white, high-heel sandals were inside.

"Wow," whispered Sarah. "These shoes have never been worn."

"No, I bought them to match the tiny white flowers in the dress."

Sarah looked doubtful. "Will I be able to *dance* in these?"

"Yes, you will, because you have no choice."

"She could wear her everyday sandals," suggested Peggy.

"Tell your mother I am in charge of this operation."

Peggy, recognizing defeat, left to find the children. "At least I still have some say-so over the younger ones," she muttered.

Sarah sat on the edge of the bed. "Granny Jewel, I'm so sorry you can't go, and that you are in pain, but I am so excited! Thank you for making it possible."

"There's only one thing I ask, my dear."

"Anything."

"Tomorrow, you must tell me every detail of your evening."

"I will, oh, I will!"

"Now, in the bottom drawer of my vanity, there is a box with an evening bag inside. You'll need it for your powder and lipstick."

"You are the very best grandma in the world," said Sarah, giving her grandmother a hug.

At eight o'clock, Sarah and her mother sat in the living room, waiting for their escorts. "Where can they be?" wondered Peggy, looking pretty in a dress of organdy and lace.

"I haven't seen either of them since supper," replied Sarah, remembering how miserable it had been, trying to eat while butterflies danced in her stomach. Soon, footsteps were heard on the front porch.

"Sit still, ladies," ordered Clara. "I will see who's at the door."

"Come in, gentlemen," they heard Clara say. Footsteps were heard in the hall and then two men dressed in black pants, white shirts and white dinner jackets appeared. Both had slicked their hair back with thick pomade, much like actors in a film.

"Oh," gasped the ladies. "Who are these handsome men? I don't believe I recognize them," declared Peggy.

"Ma'am, we have come to escort you to the dance." As if rehearsed, both clicked their heels together and bowed. Peggy and Sarah stood, and took their outstretched arms. None saw the lady of the house standing in the upstairs shadows, watching as they got into the car.

"Amy's asleep, and Joshua is in his room, playing," said a voice behind her. "I can stay if you think you'll need me."

Granny Jewel turned, "Thanks, Clara, but we'll be fine. You go on home with William. I can get about if the children need me."

"Yep," replied Clara, giving her a rare smile. "I'm sure you'll soon be good as new."

It seemed to Sarah the drive over three bridges and through Morehead City would take forever. Finally, she saw the lights from the Pavilion glowing in the night sky. When her father parked the car, music from the band could be heard above the soft pounding of the surf on the beach.

"Come on, ladies," urged her father. "There's a lot of dancing that needs to be done."

"Papa," said Sarah as she stood beside the car, smoothing her dress, "I know you're disappointed Granny Jewel couldn't come tonight."

Tom Mitchell looked at the face of his beautiful granddaughter. The soft light made her lovelier than ever. "No, my darling one, I am most fortunate and blessed. I have lived to see both my children grown and I am enjoying three precious grandchildren. Tonight, I have the pleasure of escorting my older granddaughter to her first big dance. Every eye will be on you, tonight, and I'll be the proudest man alive."

"Thank you, Papa," Sarah said squeezing her grandfather's arm. "Let's get in there and 'cut a rug.'" As they walked up the steps, Sarah wondered what it would be like to someday enter a ballroom on the arm of a tall, handsome young man. For a moment, she envisioned being on the arm of Porter Mason, as he looked down, a dark red curl falling across his forehead.

There was no opportunity for conversation. The band was playing a slow dance and the floor was filled with couples. The sweet scent of ladies' perfume mingled with the tang of salt air off the ocean. Across the room, a group of teenagers were sitting at a table.

"Hey, Marnie," called one of the boys, "isn't that girl in the green dress your cousin from Beaufort?" All eyes turned in time to see Sarah float onto the dance floor. "You'll have to introduce me," remarked the boy, never noticing the storm clouds growing on the face of the pretty blonde girl.

Hoping to win an approving glance from Marnie, the girl on her right said disapprovingly, "Her date looks old enough to be her *grandfather.*"

Marnie turned quickly, blonde curls bouncing, fists clenched. "He *is* her grandfather, you idiot!"

After several dances, the couples switched partners. "Ah," said her father, whirling her across the floor in a fox trot, "I have wanted to dance with the lovely lady in green all evening."

"Don't let your date hear you," whispered Sarah, smiling. "She might get jealous."

During intermission, the band director placed a large, gold trophy on the podium. "Ladies and gentlemen, may I have your attention." The crowd slowly quieted. "It is the custom at many dances to have a contest to see which couple is the best dancer. Tonight, our dance category is 'jitter bug'. Grab your partner and catch your breath, because we're about to begin."

"Hey, honey," said James, as Peggy sat down heavily in a chair at their table. "You can't quit now. The contest is about to begin." Sarah, sitting across from her parents, grinned at her father. He sounded desperate.

Peggy Bowers wearily brushed a strand of hair from her forehead. "James, my feet are killing me. These high heel sandals are pretty, but not very good for dancing." She darted a look at her daughter sitting across from her.

"Why don't you ask your daughter? This would be an excellent chance for you all to use some of those fancy steps you've been practicing at home."

James looked hopefully at his daughter. "What about it, Sissie? Do you think we could show these folks a thing or two on the dance floor?"

Sarah looked hopefully at her grandfather. "I don't know, Daddy. You'll have to ask my date. He may want to be in the contest."

Papa Tom quickly waved his hands in protest. "Sorry kids, this old man needs a break. You two go ahead and I'll sit and keep your wife company."

The voice of the announcer interrupted. "All couples for the jitter bug contest please come up and get a number."

James Bowers quickly removed his dinner jacket and hung it over the back of a chair. He unfastened his black bow tie, threw it on the table and grabbed Sarah's hand. "Come on, Sissie. There isn't a minute to lose." Sarah could feel herself being pulled onto the dance floor. There were several couples ahead of them picking numbered cards which were pinned on the gentleman's back. James chose the number three. "This is our lucky number, honey."

"What's lucky about the number three?"

James gave his daughter a hug. "Because, I have three beautiful children."

The couples spaced themselves on the dance floor, allowing room to execute the vigorous whirls and dips.

The familiar music from Tommy Dorsey's "Boogie-Woogie" suddenly filled the high, raftered ceiling. The rhythm was lively and the beat strong. People sitting or standing nearby tapped their hands or feet to the pulsing rhythm.

Sarah and her father began with Sarah in his arms, keeping time with the music by swaying and tapping their feet. James placed his hand at Sarah's back and guided her away with one hand while she ducked under his other arm. After several minutes, Sarah said breathlessly, "Daddy, these high heel sandals were not meant for this kind of dancing. I'm afraid I'm holding you back."

"Kick them off, honey," answered her father as he expertly twirled his daughter."

"Do you think that would be against the rules?"

"I don't think so, after all, we're on the beach, and people go barefoot on the beach." The offending shoes were quickly kicked off, landing under a nearby table.

"This is great, Daddy," she said, twirling past her father. "It's like dancing in the living room." With her feet free, Sarah could concentrate on her steps and not worry about the possibility of falling. Unconcerned about the couples around them, father and daughter laughed and danced, people on the sidelines, a blur. *I hope Granny Jewel's dress doesn't get torn*, thought Sarah fleetingly. The full skirt swirled around her legs, occasionally showing her leg as far as the knee.

The music stopped. On the last note, the girl almost collapsed in her father's arms. While the music played, it was impossible to be still, now in the silence, dancers were trying to catch their breath. The band leader came to the microphone. "Let's give all the contestants a big hand, folks," he instructed. "Now comes the hard part." He looked out over the dance floor. "Everyone did a great job dancing the 'jitter bug'. Some of you could dance on stage in New York City. However, the couple that seemed to be having the finest time and really enjoying themselves, was the father-daughter team from Beaufort, couple number 3!" The other dancers parted as Sarah and her father made their way to the stage. The crowd was a blur of people applauding and smiling for the winning couple.

"The judges were impressed when this little lady kicked off her shoes and got down to the business of having a good time."

"Go up and get your trophy," said James in her ear.

"You come too, Daddy," said Sarah, suddenly feeling self conscious about her bare feet.

"You earned it, Sarah."

Sarah gathered the bottom of her skirt, and quickly mounted the steps to the stage. When the band leader handed her the gold trophy, the audience once more applauded. Sarah glanced over at the table where her mother and grandfather were sitting. They were smiling and clapping furiously.

"James, you and Sarah were magnificent!" exclaimed Peggy as Sarah put the heavy trophy in the middle of the table. The base was made of marble, with gold columns, a couple dancing on top.

"I can't believe it!" laughed Sarah. "There were some very good dancers on the floor."

"The difference, my dear girl," said her grandfather, "was the fact that the other couples were concentrating on their moves, and you two were enjoying yourselves."

"I want to dance with my daughter," said Papa Tom, when the band played a slow song. He held his hand out to Peggy. "I'm sure we're no match for our family members, but we can try our best," he said giving his granddaughter a broad wink.

James turned to Sarah. "Why don't we step out on the boardwalk and enjoy the cool breeze."

"That's a good idea, Daddy." Sarah found her shoes and quickly put them on. Strangers continued to congratulate her as she walked through the clusters of people.

Outside, the cool breeze felt wonderful on their skin. The music was fainter, making it possible to hear the waves thunder and pound against the creamy white sand of the beach. "I think we need a cold drink, don't you? I'll go inside and find two glasses of iced tea. We can drink them out here with stars, a new moon and ghost crabs as our audience."

"That sounds good, Daddy." James hurried inside, while Sarah turned her attention to the stars overhead.

A strident voice interrupted her thoughts. "Well, my, my, if it isn't the famous Ginger Rogers taking the evening air."

Sarah rolled her eyes, turning slowly toward the voice. "Hello, Marnie. I didn't know you were here."

Marnie, followed by her date and several others, walked slowly toward Sarah. Her smile was more of a grimace, her eyes resembled those of a shark moving in for the kill.

"Of course you didn't know I was here, you were busy on the dance floor."

The others laughed nervously. Marnie ignored them.

"Are you trying to start a new fad by dancing barefoot? I suppose you think everybody will kick their shoes off now."

"I haven't given it a single thought, Marnie. I kicked mine off because they hurt my feet. It's as simple as that."

The others laughed and Sarah smiled. Marnie scowled.

"Where on earth did you find that dress? Did someone buy it for you?" Surely you didn't select it." Marnie took a step closer.

"No, Marnie, I didn't." Sarah looked down at her lovely dress, shimmering in the soft glow from the lighted dance floor. "It's my grandmother's dress. She was kind enough to let me wear it tonight."

Marnie put her hands on her hips and tilted her head to one side. "How nice," she said sarcastically. "We were not that lucky," she said, nodding at her friends. "We shopped for hours to find the perfect dress, didn't we, girls?" Silence followed her remark.

Marnie, sensing her friends' disapproval, leveled one final remark. "I won't be in boring Beaufort, this summer. My family's staying in a cottage on the beach." With that, she whirled around and started inside.

Several remarks were dancing on the tip of Sarah's tongue, but she pressed her lips in a thin line and said nothing, determined not to let her mean spirited cousin ruin her evening. One of the young men hung back, acting nervous. "I thought your dancing was great, and I think your dress is pretty."

He took a deep breath, but before he could speak, Marnie's voice split the air. *"Walter!"* she yelled. The young man bolted, running to catch up with the others.

Seconds later, James appeared with two tall glasses of iced tea. "Were you talking to someone, honey? I thought I heard voices."

Smiling up at her father, Sarah answered, "You must have heard the squawking of a sea gull, Daddy."

At church the following morning, Sarah was congratulated by couples who had attended the dance. However, Sarah didn't capture all the limelight. People were amazed at how quickly Jewel Mitchell had recovered from her frightful accident. She took her usual place in the choir loft, after processing the aisle with scarcely a limp. All agreed she was a remarkable woman, a most remarkable woman.

Chapter 10

Joshua slid along the cool, dark pew at St. Paul's Episcopal Church. He knew the next sixty minutes would tax his strength and concentration. The pews were so horribly uncomfortable a person had to remain conscious the whole service, or run the chance of dozing and pitching headlong in the floor. Before his parents could be seated, he heard his name whispered by someone sitting in the pew behind him. Quickly he turned before his mother had a chance to give him a disapproving look. From the corner of his eye, he saw Katie Higgins sitting between her parents.

"I want to ask you something," she said in a whisper. He could only nod before he got the look he was expecting.

During the long service, Joshua passed the time wondering what Katie wanted. The summer vacation was almost half over, and he had seen her only on Sunday mornings. *It must be something really important, or she wouldn't have whispered in church.* After what seemed an endless time, the choir recessed, the minister gave the benediction, and the service was over.

Joshua leaned over the pew which had held him captive, and spoke. "Hi, Katie," he said. "What did you want to ask me?"

Katie Higgins, blonde hair framing her face, looked solemnly at Joshua through big, brown eyes. "I can't talk here, so, can you come over to my house this afternoon?"

Joshua remembered the fun he and Katie had the summer before, playing on the island where her father was director of the U.S. Fish and Wildlife Laboratory. On Sunday afternoons they could run, swim and climb trees, instead of sitting quietly all afternoon as he was compelled to do in town. He quickly relayed Katie's invitation to his mother, squeezing her hand for good measure.

"Please, Mama, can I go. Katie needs me."

The parents agreed, Peggy and James promising to bring Joshua over after Sunday dinner. "Joshua can come home with us," said Katie's mother, smiling.

"Do you want to go home with Katie?" asked his father.

Joshua pictured himself climbing a silver maple tree with his good clothes and shoes with slippery soles. In a matter of minutes he'd slide off a bough and land on the ground. Katie's laughter from the summer before, echoed in his mind. It would be pure torture to wear his Sunday clothes all day. Besides, it was hard enough to keep up with Katie when he was wearing sneakers and shorts. "I'll wait," he said. "Katie will just have to be patient." He didn't see his mother roll her beautiful blue eyes.

"I think it would be fun to live on an island," offered Joshua, sitting between his parents in his father's truck. When they turned off the causeway and drove across the narrow bridge, Joshua felt a sense of excitement. He looked up at the old laboratory as they drove past. Not even the bright summer sun could erase the spooky appearance of the old building, with its porches and strange shaped cupolas.

As they drove in the Higgins' driveway, Katie's face appeared on the driver's side. After greetings, Katie drew the boy aside. "There's something I want to show you," she declared, pulling Joshua toward the back yard. He turned in time to see his parents going in Katie's house.

"What is it, Katie?" he asked.

"Don't talk. Just follow me."

Joshua, becoming irritated, replied, "What is so mysterious about a back yard? Everybody has one."

Katie stopped suddenly. "Not everybody has a back yard like mine. This whole island is my back yard. If you don't want to see something wonderful, tell me, and we can go inside and sit with the grown ups and be polite."

Joshua thought about being trapped inside on a pretty day, trying to sit still and remember his manners. "Lead on, Katie. I promise not to say another word."

Katie hurried through the yard, Joshua close behind. When they came to a rusty gate, Katie slipped through. "Be careful not to get cut on rusty wire," she cautioned. "You could get lockjaw and die." Joshua, fearing such a terrible death, avoided the pieces of gate that were covered with the brown crust.

Suddenly, Katie eased down on thick, green grass and remained motionless. Joshua sat beside her, wondering why they had stopped. Afraid to ask, he strained his eyes to see what Katie's gaze was fixed upon. A mosquito buzzed in his ear. Without thinking, he slapped at the offending insect. This brought a disapproving scowl from his companion.

This is a waste of time, Joshua decided. *Why should I sit here and be eaten by gnats, mosquitoes and ants while she stares at a clump of bushes. I don't care if there is a two headed dragon in there, it can't be as bad as a six-legged bug.* He opened his mouth to tell Katie he was going to the house when he heard a slight rustling in the bushes. Glancing quickly at Katie, he saw only her eyes blink. "Look, Joshua," she whispered so faintly, he barely heard. Staring straight ahead, he saw a brown head peep out of the thick bushes. It was followed by a body covered in brown feathers.

Oh, great, thought the boy. It's a duck. Big deal. There are plenty of them in Pullen Park in Raleigh. The duck was quacking softly and moving away from the underbrush. A tiny duckling, covered in brown and gold fuzz, followed. More ducklings appeared, following their mother. In a straight line, she led them to the nearby shore. When they were out of sight, Joshua asked, "Where is she taking them, Katie?"

"She's leading them to water. She'll teach them how to find bugs and minnows." Katie stood, followed by Joshua who vigorously brushed his shorts, making sure no ant had lost his way and was crawling around inside his underwear.

"They sure are cute. Can I have one for a pet? Little Chick, my pet chicken, would love some company."

Katie frowned and shook her head. "I don't think so. My daddy doesn't like to see animals in pens. He says they need to be free."

"Animals can't be free in town."

"That's terrible," replied Katie.

"In the city, there are laws about keeping animals."

"That's even more terrible. I couldn't live in a place like that. I think I'd dry up and blow away."

"Well, I never heard of anybody in Raleigh drying up. Besides, what are you going to do when you get married and move away?"

"I'm going to marry a cowboy and ride horses every day."

Joshua felt a sudden twinge of jealousy. "I have been thinking about being a cowboy, just like Roy Rogers and having a horse like Trigger."

Katie laughed merrily. Joshua noticed she was almost pretty when she smiled. The moment was shattered when she blurted, "You on a horse? You wouldn't last five minutes before you'd be on the ground. You're a city boy, and city boys don't know anything about ranches and cattle and stuff like that."

Joshua's first desire was to knock her down and watch the gleeful look disappear. However, he knew the terrible price he'd pay if she hurried inside and told what he'd done. Somehow, he didn't think she'd tattle. To change the subject, he asked, "What did you want to ask me, Katie. I don't have all day, you know."

Katie, still smiling, suddenly grabbed Joshua's hand. "Come on, I'm going to take you to my secret hiding place. You have to promise you'll never tell a single soul where it is." Katie's solemn expression had returned.

"I promise, Katie." Together they walked around the laboratory, past the terrapin pens and behind the aquarium which housed tanks of undersea life. When they got to the foot of the single car bridge, Katie looked quickly to see that no one was around. Satisfied, she scrambled over huge boulders that led down to the water and disappeared under the bridge, looking back to make sure Joshua was close behind. Trying not to lose his footing and fall among sharp oyster rocks, Joshua climbed over the boulders and under the edge of the bridge. When he looked up, he saw Katie perched on a flat rock high above, smiling down. "Welcome to my hidden room," she whispered.

Joshua scrambled over rocks and joined her. Shade from the bridge, made the room cool. Waves gently lapped against the oyster rocks below. Pigeons, sitting on bridge girders, cooed their displeasure at having their privacy challenged.

"This is better than a tree house, Katie," said Joshua enthusiastically. "You are so lucky to live on an island and have a camp like this." He was rewarded with one of her shy smiles.

Joshua settled back against the hard surface of a granite boulder. "Now, ask me the question. I'm really getting curious."

Katie didn't answer right away, but studied a hole in the canvas of her worn sneaker. Finally, she blurted, "My mama is going to have a baby."

Joshua gave her a curious look. "What's so bad about that? Lots of women have babies. It's where we got Amy."

Katie hugged her legs, resting her chin on her knees. "It's always been mama, daddy, and me; nobody else. Now this baby is going to come along and mess up everything."

"Everything does change, and babies are messy, but you get used to them after awhile."

Katie laid her hand on Joshua's arm. "I'm afraid my parents won't love me as much when the baby comes. Suppose they give all their time and love to this new person." Katie paused, looking at Joshua, "I'm thinking about running away."

Joshua turned, their faces inches apart. "Wow, Katie. Are you really serious?"

"Sure, why not? Maybe my parents will miss me and be sorry they ever thought about having another child." Katie pressed her lips together, looking defiant.

"Are you going to wait until the baby comes, or leave now?"

"Neither, I guess. I'm not allowed to leave the island by myself."

"Oh." After several minutes of silence, Joshua said, "You know, Katie, you may find out the baby isn't so bad after all. I *never* wanted a baby sister. I thought my mama would have a boy, and I'd have a brother and we could go hunting and fishing. Instead, Mama brought home a baby girl. Neighbors came over, gurgling and squeaking, trying to make her smile. I'd smile, but nobody was looking at me, they were all bent over her bassinette."

"It must have been awful. Why didn't you run away? Then your parents would be sorry they ignored you for someone new."

Joshua looked down at the water lapping at the rocks below. The tide was coming in, slowly inching closer to the pair. "If I left, who would be Amy's big brother? Who would protect her from the cold, cruel world?"

"You're joking, aren't you?"

"No, I'm not! Being an older brother or sister is very serious, and a big responsibility. Sarah helped take care of me when I was little, and she still protects me if I get hurt, or if somebody wants to beat me up."

"Do you think I'll make a good big sister?"

"You're the only choice the baby has." Joshua thought this new member of her family better learn how to climb trees and swim like a fish, very early in life.

"I don't know anything about taking care of a baby. I think I could dress one if it didn't struggle. But, I could never change a diaper. That's when I *really* would run away, permission or not."

Joshua sat up very straight and looked at his companion. "Oh, yes, you'll *have* to change diapers."

"Did you ever change a diaper?"

"Of course not!" He sniffed. "That's women's work. Men never change diapers."

"You're not a man!" Katie's hands, now clenched, were dangerously close to Joshua's nose.

"OK, OK, maybe your mother will do all the changing, but you can help by handing her stuff, like pins and baby powder. You can watch the baby while your mother hangs diapers on the clothes line. You have to wash a ton of diapers every day, because babies leak a lot."

A companionable silence followed, as Katie absorbed the information given by her by her more experienced friend.

"We'd better go back to the house," Katie suggested after several moments.

"Oh, don't forget about feeding a baby. You spoon horrible looking goo in its mouth, and the baby spits it out. It's like a game, except that the score is usually seven to nothing, in the baby's favor. He'll get food on his clothes, the high chair, the floor, and especially on you. I soon learned to let Amy make a horrible mess, so mama didn't ask me to feed her anymore." Joshua grinned. "After the baby has eaten, you have to hose off the high chair, the floor, and the baby, especially the baby."

"I hope you're kidding," said Katie, alarmed.

Joshua grinned. "Sure, I'm kidding about the hose." Under his breath he muttered, "But I'm not kidding about the rest."

On the way home, Joshua felt content. He sat between his parents and remembered the days when they had a new baby in the house. Thank goodness all that was behind them. Suddenly, fear clutched his heart. "Mama," he asked alarmed, "You aren't going to bring any more babies home are you? I mean, aren't three children enough?"

Peggy smiled at her son. "God blessed your father and me with three fine, healthy children. I hope He continues blessing us with the absence of any more."

She leaned over and smiled at his father, then gave her son a hug. For a few moments he thought of how grand it must be to be an only child. He closed his eyes and grinned as the truck crossed the bridge into Beaufort. Katie Higgins was in for a big shock, a mighty big shock.

"It looks like you're quite popular today, son," remarked James Bowers, parking in front of his in-law's home. "Isn't that your friend Mackie sitting on the front porch?"

Joshua looked up. Sure enough, Mackie was sitting in a rocking chair, reading a comic book. "Where you been?" he asked.

"Uh, I went visiting with my parents." He knew better than to say he had been playing with a girl. Mackie may decide he needed to be toughened up a bit, or worse, Mackie would be disappointed in him. Life sure was complicated.

"I got a dime. Let's go downtown and buy a comic book."

Joshua, relieved that Mackie needed no more details of his afternoon, replied, "Come up to my room and I'll get some money out of my piggy bank. We'll each have one, read it, and trade."

Mackie followed Joshua upstairs. After shaking the glass pig for some time, a dime fell out. "Come on, Joshua. I'm getting tired of waiting." Mackie stomped out, Joshua hurrying behind.

"Daddy," he called as they hurried down the stairs, "I'm going downtown with Mackie to buy a comic book." There was no answer. James Bowers was well into an afternoon nap.

"How come you have to tell somebody where you're going?"

Joshua thought a minute. "I guess my family wants to know where I'll be if they need me."

"My daddy don't ask, and I don't tell. He figures I can take care of myself."

If I disappeared, thought Joshua, *my parents, sisters, and grandparents would be out searching. Clara would come armed with her wooden stirring spoon, ready to do battle.* It was a comforting thought.

The selection of comic books was better at Guthrie-Jones drug store. One wall was devoted to that month's latest magazines. After carefully thumbing every book, the boys decided on Captain Marvel and Batman. Each paid the clerk and stepped out in the afternoon heat.

"Let's go to my house," suggested Mackie.

"Sure, then you can come home with me for supper."

The boys had to tip toe past Mr. Fuller, sleeping peacefully on the sofa, a radio playing soft music. When they reached Mackie's room, Joshua watched horrified as the older boy pulled up the front of his shirt, showing several comics tucked in the front of his shorts. He grinned. "What do you think? I made a pretty good haul, didn't I? Did you lift any?"

Joshua stepped back. His friend stood, proudly holding up three comic books he had not paid for. He took a step back toward the door. "How did you do that?" he asked incredulously. "I never saw you hide even one."

"It takes practice, kid, lots of practice. I'll show you how it's done." Mistaking Joshua's silence for approval, he continued, "It's a lot easier in the winter, when you're wearing a coat. It's tougher in the summer time." Mackie laughed. "First thing you have to do is check to make sure . . . ."

"Stop!" yelled Joshua. "I don't want to hear any more." He put his hands over his ears. Mackie's mouth dropped open, eyes wide with surprise. "You know stealing is wrong. It's a sin. It's one of the Ten Commandments."

Mackie's expression faded, replaced with anger. "I should have known 'sissy boy' wouldn't approve." He pounded a fist in the palm of his hand. "You better not tell, or you'll be sorry." Slowly he moved toward the smaller boy.

Joshua's first impulse was to run. However, he stood his ground, knowing soon he would be a grease spot on the floor. Mackie moved closer, expecting Joshua to turn and run. He could see beads of perspiration on Mackie's face, every freckle easy to count.

Joshua swallowed hard. "We're supposed to be friends! If you had been caught, I'd be in trouble, too. I don't want you for my friend anymore. Stay away from me!" The smaller boy squeezed his eyes shut, waiting. A blow to his left jaw caused Joshua to lose his balance and fall.

"Hey, what's going on in there?" came a voice from the living room.

"It ain't nothing, Daddy, Joshua just lost his balance," yelled Mackie.

Joshua, on his feet in an instant, backed toward the door, swung it open and hurried through the house and out the back door. Fearing he would get stuck in the fence opening between their yards, he hurried around the side of the house and out to the sidewalk. Mackie stepped out on his front porch. "That's right, Sissy Boy. Run home and tell your mama."

"If I'm a 'sissy boy,' then you're a bully! Bullies always pick on somebody smaller. Next time, pick on somebody your own size!"

Mackie moved toward the porch steps. When he did, Joshua turned and with wings on his sneakers, flew down the block to the corner, turned sharply by grabbing a fence post, and continued until he reached the next corner. He slowed enough to look back, relieved that Mackie had not followed. He looked down at his new comic book, clutched in his fist, the corners already frayed. He turned onto Ann Street, breathing rapidly, and slowed his pace. *I'm never going to hang around with him again*, the boy vowed. When he reached the safety of his grandparent's front porch, he was flooded with relief. He opened the screen door quietly, and crept up the stairs, listening to his father's contented snoring in the room below. Thankfully, no one was in the bathroom at that moment. He stared at his reflection, watching a bruise spread across his left cheek. Suddenly, his vision blurred as unbidden tears flooded his eyes. He buried his face in a wash cloth before the sobs came. As quickly as they began, the tears were over. Soon, he was able to wet the cloth in cold water and wash his face. "I hate him," he muttered over and over. "I hope the police go to his house and arrest him, handcuffs and all. Maybe they'll keep him in jail the rest of his life, and only give him bread and water to eat."

"Joshua, are you in the bathroom?" came his mother's voice. "Who are you talking to?"

"Nobody, Mama."

"Well, hurry, son. Mackie's waiting for you on the front porch."

Joshua's eyes, the size of saucers and red as an autumn sunset, stared at his reflection. His hand trembled on the door knob. Looking down the stairs, he saw a familiar outline pressed against the screen door. It was Mackie. Was he brave enough to kill someone in their own home? Would his daddy wake up in time to hear his son's last gasp?

His mother appeared at the bottom of the steps, smiling. He had never noticed before how beautiful his mother was. She had always just looked like Mama. He would miss her up in Heaven. "Hurry, Honey. You can't expect Mackie to wait all day."

"I got to talk to you," Mackie whispered through the screen. Joshua felt encouraged. At least he hadn't said, "I got to kill you."

"What do you want?" whispered Joshua.

"I can't talk through the door, Joshua. Come out here on the porch."

Joshua slid through the door and out onto the porch. "Look," said Mackie, looking uncomfortable. "I know I shouldn't have punched you. I'm sorry, I think."

"You shouldn't have stolen those comic books. That makes you a thief. I'm not going to hang around with a thief."

Mackie slumped in a rocking chair. "I won't do it again, at least, not any time soon."

"That's not good enough. You need to give up stealing for good."

Mackie appeared deep I thought. "OK, for good." He said finally.

Joshua stood in front of Mackie's chair, hands on hips. "You got to go to the drug store and pay for the ones you took."

"I ain't about to do that."

"You have to do it to make it right."

Mackie slumped farther down in the chair, defeated. "Where am I going to get money for comics every month?"

"You can start by helping me clean the back yard of my uncle's new house. We can do it together so it won't take as long, and we'll have enough money for lots of comics."

Mackie looked doubtul. "Yeah, but, where am I going to get the money for these?" He pulled the comic books from his back pocket.

"I still have money in my piggy bank. I'll give you the thirty cents, and go with you to the drug store."

"No way."

"Good-bye, Mackie." Joshua turned to go inside.

"OK, OK," the older boy said quickly. "I'll do it."

The drug store clerk, busy with customers, accepted the three dimes without looking up from the cash register.

"I brought an extra dime," said Joshua. "Let's get a cold Coca-Cola to celebrate.

Walking slowly down the tree lined street, enjoying the cool ocean breeze, Mackie turned to his friend, "Paying for stuff sure is going to be boring."

"Your mama would be proud of you," answered Joshua, sipping the cold sweet liquid through a paper straw.

Mackie nodded, a smile spreading across his face. "Yeah, you're right. Mama would be mighty proud of me."

Chapter 11

Bars of golden sunlight sifted through gently moving lace curtains. The family was enjoying a late supper of cold fried chicken, potato salad, string beans and hot rolls. An extra place had been set for Mackie who was taking advantage of an opportunity to enjoy Clara's cooking.

Peggy, glancing at her son, raised her eyebrows. "Joshua," she asked, "did you wash your face before you came to the table?"

Joshua, quickly turning the left side of his face away from his mother. "Yes, Ma'am," he replied. He hurriedly stuffed his cheeks with potato salad so he wouldn't have to answer more questions, learning early in life that talking with food in your mouth would not be tolerated.

Sarah, from the opposite side, remarked, "It's a dark patch on his jaw." Turning to her brother, she asked, "Where did you get that bruise? Did you try to stop a train with the side of your face?"

"Make her stop, Mama," was his muffled reply, still working on the potato salad.

"I'm curious, too, Son," added his father. "Tell us how it happened."

Joshua, being careful not to look at his friend, replied, "Can't a person have a bruise without everybody having to know what happened? Can't a guy have a secret *sometime*?"

From the look on James Bower's face, Mackie realized his friend was wading into treacherous water. "I hit him, Mr. Bowers. I socked him so hard he landed on the floor."

Mackie's voice faded, replaced by silence. He slowly placed his fork in his plate and looked at Granny Jewel. "Thanks for supper, Mrs. Mitchell. I guess I'll be leaving now." Slowly he stood, glancing longingly at the delicious food still on his plate.

"Oh, no, young man," said Granny Jewel. "You must ask permission to leave the table in this house. Besides, you haven't cleaned your plate. Think of the starving orphans in Europe who would give anything to eat the scraps from our tables."

"Yes Ma'am," he answered, not meeting her gaze. He sighed deeply. "Do I have permission to leave?"

"Certainly not! You have to stay for lemon pie. What would happen if Clara found out that you refused a slice of her pie?"

"That would be really bad for me." Mackie sat down, but before he picked up his fork, his eyes traveled around the table. "What happened was, I swiped some comic books from the drug store, and Joshua told me I had to go back and pay for them. I knew he was right, but I didn't want to do it, so, I socked him hard so he'd go away. After he left I felt bad, cause he's the only friend I got. I came over here to tell him I'd pay, if I wasn't broke. So, he got the money out of his piggy bank and we went downtown and I paid the clerk thirty cents."

Again silence filled the room. After a few moments, Papa Tom asked, "How did you feel after you paid for the comics?"

"I felt good, because I knew a policeman wouldn't be grabbing me by the collar."

"Mackie, did it make you feel good inside to know you had done the right thing?" asked Granny Jewel

"Yeah," he said, a slow grin spreading. "It did feel a little bit good."

"Mama," interrupted Joshua, "Mackie and I are going to ask Uncle Herb if we can rake the yard at his new house."

"I know he'd be glad for someone else to do it. August is almost here and the house isn't near ready. They have to be out of the apartment in two weeks. I don't know how they're going to do it."

"Now, don't you worry, dear," comforted Papa Tom. "We won't let our children sleep on the street." He winked at the boys. "They can sleep upstairs over the grocery store."

Before the grandmother could reply, the telephone rang. "I'll get it," said Sarah, jumping up. "Oh, may I have permission to leave the table?" she asked, winking at her grandmother.

Granny Jewel sniffed. "Yes dear, you may. It's probably Bruce."

"Sarah?"

"Oh, Nancy! I'm so glad you're back! I have lots to tell you. Can you come over?"

"Hmmm, not tonight. My parents want me to stay home because I've been gone all summer."

"Did you come home on the bus?"

"No, Mama and Daddy came and picked me up. To take a bus from Greensboro to Beaufort would take all day."

"Can you come down to the store tomorrow? Bring a sandwich and we'll eat lunch on the dock where we can talk in private."

On Monday at exactly twelve o'clock, Nancy stepped in the front door of Mitchell's Grocery, a brown paper bag in hand. "Nancy Russert, you haven't changed one bit," exclaimed Sarah from behind the candy counter.

"And look at you," remarked Nancy as Sarah stepped from behind the huge wooden pickle barrel. "I declare, you're taller than ever! If you keep on, no boy under six feet will ask you for a date." Both girls laughed as they embraced.

"Hello, Nancy," called Herb Mitchell from behind the butcher counter. "How is my favorite dance instructor?"

"I'm fine, Mr. Mitchell, and glad to be home. There's no ocean breeze in Greensboro."

"I'll bet not. It would have to blow mighty hard to be felt that far inland."

"Uncle Herb, Nancy and I are going to eat lunch on the government dock. I'll be back in an hour unless you need me before then."

"Take an extra long lunch, Sarah. It's a slow day, and I know you two have a lot of catching up to do." He dismissed them with a wave of his hand.

"Let's sit on the end of the dock and stick our toes in the water."

Sarah followed her friend, more than willing to kick off her shoes and cool her feet in the clear blue-green salt water. For a moment they were busy unwrapping sandwiches, tucking the wax paper wrappers between the cracks in the dock. "If we don't anchor the paper, it'll blow all the way to Ann Street," laughed Sarah, letting the breeze toss her hair.

"Tell me about your summer, first," said Nancy between tiny bites of a chicken salad sandwich.

Sarah bit thoughtfully into a fried bologna sandwich. Clara had removed the rag from around the meat early that morning and fried a thick slice for her sandwich. Mustard and mayonnaise made the sandwich complete. "Hmmm, I don't know where to begin. I guess I could start with the morning after we got here. I went sailing with Bruce."

"Did you sail out to the inlet?"

"No, he decided to stay in Taylor's Creek since he caught my grandfather spying on us from the street."

"Did he kiss you?"

"No, Nancy. He did not kiss me in the broad daylight with Papa Tom and Joshua watching from the shore."

"Has he kissed you?" asked Nancy, uninterested in any details concerning sailing.

"Of course, silly. If we're old enough to drive a car, we're old enough to be kissed."

"I agree, but my daddy thinks I'll have a wreck as soon as I get under the wheel. Fathers are too protective. I don't think they want us to ever have any fun." Nancy kicked her feet furiously in the water, showering them with drops.

"I went to the big dance at the Pavilion on Atlantic Beach."

"Oh?" Nancy, eager to hear details, stared at her friend.

"I'll bet Bruce looked handsome. Is he a good dancer?"

"I didn't go with Bruce." Sarah smiled at her friend.

"What? Who did you go with? Do I know him?" Nancy shook Sarah's arm, almost causing her to drop the remainder of her sandwich.

"I'll give you a hint. He's tall, dark and handsome, *and* he's out of high school." Sarah looked serious. "He says he loves me very much, and truthfully, I love him, too."

"Where does Bruce fit in this very lovely picture?" Nancy tossed the remainder of her sandwich in the water and watched as the crust was gobbled up by tiny silver fish.

"Bruce and I are going steady, but . . ." Sarah showed Nancy her heart shaped necklace, "he didn't mind if I went to the dance with Papa Tom." Sarah burst out laughing, joined by her friend. After filling Nancy in on all the details of the dance, she asked, "How was your summer? Did you meet any cute boys?"

Nancy stared at the islands across the channel. "I met a lot of cute boys, but, I have to be true to Henry. Everybody was dedicated to their music. Most of the kids practice as much as eight hours a day. Some were considered geniuses."

Sarah detected a note of sadness in her friend's voice.

"Hey, none of them can be more dedicated than you. I've heard you play, and nobody can be better than you."

"Thanks, Sarah," Nancy said quietly, "but I was in the presence of people with talent I can only imagine. The worst part is they're *my* age. If they are that good now, they'll be concert pianists after college. I'm afraid hard work can't always substitute for ability."

"Seriously, Nancy, you can be anything you want to be. With your dedication, I know some day you'll play with the North Carolina symphony. I'll take my kids to concerts, and say, 'see the lady at the piano, wearing a black dress? She and I used to sit on the end of a dock, soak our feet in salt water and eat sandwiches.'"

"I did win an award," said Nancy shyly. "On the last day, after all the scholarships and awards were given, they presented me with a tiny gold piano for 'dedication, determination and meticulous execution.'"

"See? What did I tell you! Someday you will be famous, and I'll be, I'll be, uh, no telling where."

"You'll know what you want to do when the time comes," declared Nancy.

"Say," interrupted Sarah, changing the subject, "let's give a party! I've been waiting for you to get home so we could do it together."

Nancy clasped her hands. "I love parties! Where do we begin?"

"Well, my friend Emily at the Duchess beauty parlor is getting married this month. From the way she talked, she and Kevin won't have much to start housekeeping. Most of their money will go for rent and groceries. I thought it would be nice if we gave her a shower so she will have sheets and a toaster and all that stuff."

"That's a great idea! It can be a miscellaneous shower. That way, she can get all kinds of gifts. We can serve tiny sandwiches, mints, nuts, and punch with slivers of ice." Nancy paused. "Where are we going to have the party?"

"Oh, my granny said we could have it at her house."

"Are you sure?" asked Nancy, doubt in her voice.

"Yes, I'm sure. If Granny Jewel said it, it's written in stone."

Nancy carefully folded her paper bag and put it in the pocket of her shorts. "Let's go ask Mama just to make sure." As they stepped off the dock, Sarah glanced at her friend, puzzled at her expression.

Sarah remained silent while her friend tried to discuss party plans with Mrs. Cora. "It doesn't sound like a good idea to me," snapped the older woman. "Emily will manage somehow. All young couples have to struggle at first."

"Why should she have to struggle when lots of ladies would be glad to give her a gift?"

Mrs. Cora turned to Sarah. "I'm sure your mother and grandmother don't approve of this idea."

"Oh, yes, Ma'am, when I mentioned it, Granny Jewel said we could have it at her house."

"Glory be!" exclaimed Mrs. Cora, sitting down hard on the edge of a dainty chair covered in flowered chintz. "Jewel Mitchell has always been a bit careless when it came to observing the rules of polite society."

Sarah, confused by the older woman's remark, couldn't think of a reply. Finally, she turned to Nancy. "I have to get back to work," she said, moving toward the door.

"I'll walk back with you," Nancy said quickly.

That evening Jewel Mitchell was standing in the hall when the telephone rang. "Hello," she said, greeting the person on the line.

"Jewel, I'm going to get right to the point," blurted Cora Russert. "What do you know about our girls wanting to give Emily at the Duchess a bridal shower?"

Before Jewel could answer, Cora continued, "I know you've tried to discourage them, and so will I."

"On the contrary, Cora, I told Sarah they could have the party here. Emily has always taken a special interest in our girls, and they think a lot of her. A shower would help with the things they need to furnish their apartment."

Mrs. Cora detected a note of determination in her friend's voice and knew from years of serving on committees with Jewel Mitchell, it would be a waste of time to try and convince her giving Emily a party could be committing social suicide. "Who do you think will come, Jewel, or rather, who will the girls invite?"

"Cora, they could start with women she transforms each week from housewives to glamorous ladies. We all feel a little bit in touch with movie stars when Emily works her magic."

"I admit it will be good practice for our girls to learn to plan a successful social event," mumbled Cora. She knew when she had been soundly defeated.

Granny Jewel replaced the receiver, turned and saw Clara standing, hands on hips. "Are you going to allow those young'uns to do what I think you're going to do?"

"And what is that, Clara?"

"You know what I'm talking about! You're exposing those innocent lambs to the likes of that loose woman. Have you forgotten she ran away with a man and not so much as a wedding band on her finger?"

Granny Jewel rolled her eyes. "Clara," she said patiently, "Emily made some mistakes, but that's all in the past. Now, she's getting married to a fine young man, and deserves a chance for a good life."

The two women took a step closer, eyes narrowing, lips pressed. "Sarah and Nancy will work their fingers to the bone, and *nobody* will come. Mark my words!"

Neither saw a face peer through the screen door. In an instant it was gone.

"What's the matter daddy? Is the screen door *hooked* ?" Herb Mitchell couldn't understand why his father was hurrying down the front steps.

"No, son. The door isn't locked. But, I feel it will be in our best interest to go to Bell's drug store and get lunch."

"Is something wrong?"

"Your mother and Clara have squared off about something, and I think fur is about to fly."

"You're right, Daddy," his son replied thoughtfully. "A ham sandwich from Bell's sounds a lot safer."

"Are you sure you want to give *me* a party?" asked Emily, a smile spreading across her face, replaced with a frown. "Are you sure it's all right with your parents?"

"Mrs. Cora doesn't mind, and Granny Jewel is looking forward to it."

For two days, the girls carefully filled out invitations. Sarah's stack grew quickly. She watched her friend form each letter, precisely on the line and no unsightly smudges. "Nancy," said Sarah, smiling from across the dining room table, "if you don't speed up, Emily will be married and rocking her first baby before the invitations are finished."

"Now Sarah, everything must be perfect. Invitations always go in the mail at least one week before the event. That way, the guests can write it on their calendar." Nancy looked thoughtful. "I hope we don't overlook anyone."

"Well, we invited all of her regular customers, ladies from her church, and the women in her family. That should do it."

When the last crisp, white envelope had been added to the stack, Granny Jewel joined the girls at the table. She had a tablet of white paper and a fountain pen. "Now, hostesses, you must decide what refreshments you want to serve."

"Gum drops and animal crackers sounds good enough to me," rose a voice from the kitchen.

Granny Jewel whispered, "Clara is only teasing, girls. I'm sure she's looking forward to the party."

"She sounds serious to me," whispered Sarah, eyes wide.

The older woman waved her hand. "Oh, you know how Clara loves to carry on," careful to not let her voice carry to the next room.

"Nuts and mints," suggested Sarah. "It wouldn't be a party without nuts and mints."

"I will make cucumber sandwiches. Mama can help me," added Nancy.

"We will need at least two sheet cakes, decorated with pink and yellow icing."

Clara stood in the door. "The guests will be mighty disappointed if you don't serve my famous cheese and sausage balls."

"Oh, yes," said Sarah, clapping her hands. "Will you make some, Clara, *please*?"

Clara sniffed loudly and raised her eyebrows. "I might. I just might if I take a notion."

"I hope you take a notion, Clara," said Nancy, hopefully. "Your cheese balls are the best in the whole country."

Granny Jewel, her back to the kitchen, winked. "Sally Carter, the girl who works for Ma Baylor, has a recipe for cheese balls. If Clara is too busy, maybe Sally could make them."

For a minute, it looked as if Clara would rise to twice her height. "Nothing Sally Carter cooks is coming in my kitchen! Why, I was cooking for this family long before that silly woman ever got herself born. I'm making the cheese balls and that's settled!"

"Clara, you're wonderful." The girls rushed to her side, giving her a hug.

"Girls, girls, we're not through. You will need fresh flowers for decorating the house, especially the dining table. For punch, perhaps the ladies of the Methodist church will loan us their silver punch bowl, glass plates and cups. We can use our white damask table cloth, and sterling flatware for serving."

When the girls were through, they put the invitations carefully on the mantle, far from the reach of little fingers and kitty paws. After the girls left, Jewel Mitchell remained at the table, chin resting on clasped hands.

"Did I hear right? You're going to use the best you own?"

Jewel Mitchell turned slowly. "Clara, Jesus met the Samaritan woman at a well. He knew about her past but it didn't keep Him from loving her. Mary Magdalene had an awful reputation. She was one of Jesus' friends. We should follow His example."

"Um-hum," muttered Clara. "You're right, Jesus loves everybody, but, no-where in the Bible does it say his mama approved of the company He kept."

By seven o'clock on the night of the bridal shower, the house smelled of fragrant flowers. An arrangement of summer daisies graced the hall table, sprays of long stemmed gladiolas adorned the mantles in the living and dining rooms. The white brocade tablecloth and magnolia blossoms were mirrored in the gleaming sides of the silver punch bowl, on loan from Methodist women. White candles in silver candlesticks gave the room a soft glow.

Nancy and Mrs. Cora arrived at seven o'clock. "We came a little early in case there are any last minute things to do," explained Nancy.

"Cora," called Granny Jewel, floating down the wide stairway, "our girls have worked their fingers to the bone getting the house ready. They have scrubbed and polished every surface." Jewel Mitchell gave each of her guests a swift hug, leaving the scent of lavender.

"Where is the rest of the family?" asked Mrs. Cora.

"Peggy went to Miriam's to help wrap a gift, and the rest have taken refuge at Herb's house. There's still a lot of renovating to do before August."

They were interrupted by a light tap on the front door. Sarah and Nancy, the official hostesses, opened the door. Emily, her mother and sister stood hesitantly. "Good evening, and welcome," said the girls, holding the door wide. For the first time, Sarah noticed Emily seemed nervous and unsure of herself. At the beauty parlor she was always smiling and confident.

"My, Emily, that is such a pretty dress," exclaimed Nancy, coaxing a smile from the young woman. "Green is the perfect color with your eyes and dark hair." Sarah recalled the summer she was twelve. Emily's hair had been bright yellow, her lipstick and nail polish shiny red. She had reminded Sarah of a glamorous movie star.

Granny Jewel and Peggy took charge of Emily's mother and sister, helping them to feel at ease. "This is a very grand home, Mrs. Mitchell," whispered Emily's mother.

"My husband built it for me as a wedding present. He wanted a big house so we could fill it with children and grandchildren. It's great in summer, but we rattle around in it during the winter."

Miriam stepped up and introduced herself. "I hope someday there will be more grandchildren so it will be noisy all year."

For thirty minutes the hostesses were busy greeting guests. Emily and her family were presented with corsages of white carnations and seated in the living room beside the window seat. Ladies in flowered summer dresses and white dress shoes filled the house, each bearing beautifully wrapped gifts which they presented to Emily. Clara, dressed in a black dress and frilly white apron, stepped from the kitchen, proudly carrying a silver tray laden with cheese balls. She stood proudly while guests rushed to sample them. Miss Nettie Blackwell, Granny Jewel's friend of many years, presided over the punch bowl, keeping cups filled with the icy fruit drink.

By eight thirty, the conversations had quieted. "Open your gifts," someone suggested. "It looks like Emily and Kevin will have enough to furnish two apartments," added another. The window seat was piled high with packages wrapped in pastel tissue paper, tied with shiny, wide bows.

Emily, fighting tears, replied, "I don't know how to thank you for your love and generosity. I'll never forget this night."

"You have to promise to keep us glamorous, Emily," said one lady.

"I just work with beauty that's already there," the girl replied. Her answer was greeted with a murmur of approval.

Nancy, in her precise penmanship, listed the gifts as Emily opened them. With each one, all exclaimed over the gift's beauty and usefulness. One gift, a wooden rolling pen, was greeted with laughter as guests suggested ways she could threaten her husband. When the tissue had been removed from the last gift, an array of shiny new treasures lined the circular window seat. Glow from the overhead light reflected in a toaster, cooking pots, and frying pans. Several sets of snow white cotton sheets and terry towels completed the picture. From behind her chair, Nancy produced one more gift.

"This is from Sarah and me," she said.

"Oh, but you gave the party," protested Emily. "You didn't need to give a gift."

The paper fell away, revealing a picture frame. Inside, the names and date of Emily and Kevin's marriage were embroidered in pastel letters. There was no mistaking Nancy's precise needlework.

"That's beautiful, Sarah," whispered Miss Nettie.

"I can't take any credit for the sewing, Miss Nettie. I had it framed at Eubanks' Studio. That was my contribution."

The older woman patted Sarah's hand. "That's quiet all right, honey. I'm going to make a quilter out of you someday."

By nine o'clock, guests began slowly moving toward the door. Emily excused herself and went to the kitchen. "Clara?" she asked timidly.

"I'm here, finishing washing the last of the dishes and cups."

"Clara, tonight has been like a dream. It's something I've heard others talk about at the beauty parlor, but I was never included. I feel so special knowing you went to the trouble to prepare your famous cheese balls. They were so delicious!"

Clara smiled at the pretty girl. "A person don't mind doing for others if their efforts are appreciated."

"I know," agreed Emily. "It's the same at the beauty parlor. Sometimes I can work my fingers to the bone fixing somebody's hair, and they forget to say a simple 'thank you'."

"Someday, I hope I can do something for you, Clara."

"You can do something for me now. You can get yourself on home, honey, and get a good night's rest, cause you gotta work tomorrow."

Joshua held the screen door for his grandfather, holding a sleeping Amy in his arms. Herb stopped in to walk Miriam home. Mrs. Cora and Nancy stayed a few minutes to discuss the party. All were seated in the living room, praising the girls for hosting their first social event.

"I'm gone," announced Clara, folding her ruffled apron. She turned to a chorus of 'thank you's' from the family.

"I'll walk you out," said Granny Jewel, hurrying behind her old friend.

"Clara, thank you for tonight. It must have been difficult, knowing how you feel about Emily."

Clara stepped out on the porch. "Emily? That girl's good people. I only hope I'm around to make cheese balls for her first baby shower."

Chapter 12

"Amy, are you sad because daddy has to go back to Raleigh?" James Bowers looked over the front porch rail at his younger daughter.

"No, no, Daddy," crooned Amy, in tears. "Granny Jewel's flowers are all droopy. They won't stand up."

James laid his newspaper aside, not surprised he never had the opportunity to read the first headline. "What seems to be the trouble with your grandmother's flowers?" he asked stepping off the porch.

Amy continued staring at the flowers. "They're all tired," she explained.

The bed of petunias, daisies, and marigolds had been bright and colorful for several weeks. Now, wearing a thick coat of dust, the plants looked weary and forlorn.

"I think the flowers need a drink of water," the father said. "They can't stand up because their roots are dry, and they're thirsty."

"Why don't we droop when we want a drink of water, Daddy?"

James Bowers sat on the grass beside his younger daughter. "When we're thirsty, we get a drink of water. Flowers can't do that. They have to stay in one spot, rooted to the ground. It's our job to see they have a drink of water. Then, they reward us by looking pretty."

For a few minutes, neither spoke as they watched a honey bee, trying to gather pollen among the droopy petals. "I'll water the flowers," declared Amy, moving toward the garden hose.

"Why don't we wait until after supper, Amy? You're not supposed to water plants in the middle of the day. It's not good for them."

"Why?"

"The water magnifies the sun's rays, making the plants even hotter."

"I don't understand."

"That's OK. I don't either, but, that's what your mother says, and she knows about plants and flowers."

They both looked up as the screen door closed. "Are you two praying for rain?" asked Granny Jewel, looking over the porch rail.

"Would rain make the flowers stand up?"

"Yes, honey. The flowers would perk up, and the grass would turn green again."

"I told Amy we'd water the flowers after supper," said James.

Granny Jewel looked worried. "I heard on the radio this drought covers most of the state. Our local paper had an article about the water level in the water towers in Beaufort and Morehead City. They are lower than they have been in twelve years. The article asked people to not water their lawns or wash their cars."

Tears filled Amy's eyes. "The flowers can have my glass of water. I'll drink Coca-Cola."

Granny Jewel rolled her eyes. "That's very thoughtful of you, honey, but you can't have a soda with your meals."

Peggy stepped on the porch, sat down and started fanning with the newspaper. "I heard a story about a drought in the west. Crops were dying in the fields and creeks were so dry the river bed had dried, leaving huge cracks."

James swung Amy up in his arms, stepped up on the porch and sat beside his wife.

"What happened?"

"Well, the people in one small town decided to meet at church and pray for rain. After the service started, someone slipped in late, and noticed not one person brought an umbrella."

Granny Jewel added, "If you want prayers answered, you have to have faith, and be patient. God answers prayer in His time, which is not necessarily our time."

The conversation continued over a lunch of chicken salad sandwiches, sliced tomatoes and corn on the cob. "These are the last of the vegetables from our garden. The drought killed the rest," said Granny Jewel.

"If we have to ration water, I'll be glad to stop taking baths," offered Joshua.

"That's my son," said James, grinning, "always ready to sacrifice his own needs for the good of others."

"If you don't take a bath every day, we'll all have to move out," said Sarah.

"Of course, we could move you to the shed and let you sleep there."

"Then the spiders would move out," added Papa Tom.

"How about washing clothes?" added Clara, serving bowls of lemon custard ice cream. "If we stopped washing dirty clothes it would save water. We could wear the same ones every day."

"After awhile, they'd be so stiff, we could stand them up in the corner when we went to bed at night, then jump in them the next morning," replied Joshua, enjoying the conversation. "You couldn't sneak up on anybody because your clothes would crackle when you walk, and . . ."

"That's enough, Joshua," said his mother. "You're being silly."

Clara, standing in the kitchen doorway turned. "Mark my words, there's gonna' come a storm something terrible. There'll be lightning, thunder and hail. The old devil is gonna' throw everything he can get his hands on at God's creatures."

"Is the debil going to hurt us?" asked Amy, her voice quavering.

"No, darling," reassured her mother, cleaning the area around Amy's high chair.

Later, Granny Jewel joined her husband in the living room. "Tom, I declare, between the devil and the drought, I hardly remember what I ate for lunch."

"I know, dear. I dread to think how quiet it will be here in a few weeks when our children return to Raleigh," Papa Tom spoke softly.

Days passed. The sky continued a brilliant blue, without a single cloud. Customers discussed the weather endlessly when they came to buy groceries. "I tell you, Tom," said Math Chapman, leaning on the door frame of the office. "This is a scary time. Why, one spark, and the woods would explode." Great puffs of gray smoke billowed from his pipe as he talked.

"It's so hot, my grandchildren aren't interested in going to the shore or going out in the boat," added Tom Mitchell.

"If something doesn't happen soon, there won't be a single crop worth harvesting in the fall." Math Chapman shook his head and turned to leave. "If we get a hurricane this year, we'll be worrying about what we're going to do with too much water."

Clara hurried along the sidewalk toward the Mitchell home. "My poor William," she murmured. "He sits on the front porch all day, rocking and watching the cars go by. I do believe he'd starve if I didn't run home and fix him that bite of lunch." Head down, so as not to stumble on the uneven sidewalk, Clara didn't notice the gradual change in the sky's color. The clear blue of morning was rapidly being replaced with a strange yellow color. The ocean breeze, which had been fresh all morning, suddenly died. Clara's stepped up on the back porch. Before going inside, she turned slowly, sniffed the air and whispered, "Something is bad wrong." She stepped to the edge of the porch and listened. The birds, usually so active and noisy, were strangely silent. "Um-hum," she said, nodding. "There's something about to happen, and I know what it is."

Once more she put her hand on the back door. Before she could open it, a distant rumble came from the direction of the Neuse River, twenty miles away. Where before there had been clear blue sky, there were towering clouds from the northwest, rapidly turning the sky the color of dark blue ink. A second rumble was heard, closer and much deeper. Clara lost no time going in the house to sound the alarm.

At the same time, Papa Tom was studying the north sky from the back door of the grocery store. "Sarah," he called.

"Yes, Papa?"

"We best be getting along home. There's some fierce weather coming, and your grandmother may need some help closing the windows. Besides, she gets mighty nervous during a thunder storm."

"I didn't know that, Papa."

"Your granny doesn't want anyone to know she's afraid of anything, but she gets real jumpy when lightning flashes and thunder rolls close by."

"I'll tell Uncle Herb we're leaving. If there's a storm, we won't have many customers."

Together, they hurried along the sidewalk, anxious to reach the house before the first drops of rain. As their feet touched the porch, a sudden clap of thunder made them rush inside.

Clara and Granny Jewel were busy closing windows. "We'll get the ones upstairs," called Papa Tom.

James was closing the windows as they got to the top of the stairs. "Peggy is trying to keep Amy from being frightened," he told them, "but I don't know how much success she's having. The thunder is getting louder each minute."

Suddenly, huge pelting raindrops poured down the windows in her grandparents' bedroom. Sarah stared, remembering the day four years ago, when her father left for the war. She watched him drive away in the rain, not knowing if she would ever see him again.

"Daddy?"

"I'm in your brother's room."

Sarah slipped her hand in his. "I'm glad you're here, Daddy."

"Hey, my big girl isn't afraid of a little thunder is she?" he asked, curious about the troubled expression on his daughter's face.

"Not as long as you're here with us."

A flash of lightning illuminated the now darkened house, followed by a deafening roll of thunder. Downstairs, Clara's voice rose above the others. "Everybody upstairs. There's not a minute to lose!"

"I can't leave Frisky outdoors. Suppose lightning strikes him."

"The Lord ain't gonna waste a perfectly good lightning bolt on that scruffy old dog," argued Clara.

This comment was followed by a heartbreaking wail from the boy. "Frisky is at the back door shivering all over. Granny Jewel, can't he come in just this once?"

"I don't suppose it will hurt anything for him to come in until the storm's past," shouted the grandmother over the sound of rain pelting against the windows.

Joshua rushed to the back door and threw it open. Frisky needed no invitation. He darted past his young master and hid under the dining room table. Joshua looked in the back yard as he struggled to close the wooden door against the force of the wind. All of his grandparents' trees were bowed by the force of the storm's powerful wind. *The trees look like they're praying,* he thought, as he securely latched the door.

"Everybody upstairs," ordered Clara, between rolls of thunder. Like a shepherd, Clara herded the family upstairs and into the grandparents' bedroom. "Climb on the bed," she said, "and get your feet up off the floor. If lightning hits the chimney, a ball of fire will come down and roll across the floor, destroying anything in its path."

Eight sat silently on the large, four poster bed, watching and listening. It was as if the lightning was all about them, thunder crashing after every flash. Amy whimpered in her father's arms, too afraid to cry.

After one flash, the sound of glass breaking and wood splintering could be heard downstairs. The family, alarm etched on every face, looked at each other.

"What was that, Tom?" cried Granny Jewel.

"Maybe I should go and see."

"Nobody leaves this bed," barked Clara. "After the storm, there'll be plenty of time to check for damage."

Slowly, the storm grew less violent. Lightning flashes were farther apart, and the roll of thunder was a distant, disgruntled rumble.

Afraid they would get up too soon, Clara said, "I remember my granny telling about a storm like this. It was during the Civil War and the town had been taken over by the Yankees." It was evident she had captured the family's attention, so she hurried on. "My granny was the property of Mr. and Mrs. Higgins, who lived around the corner. My granny may have been a slave, but she could be bossy at times."

"Hmmm, just like someone I know," said Papa Tom, quickly silenced by a look.

"So what happened, Clara? Did lightning strike a Yankee soldier?" asked Joshua, hopefully.

"No, honey, but the storm did drive one of them up on the front porch. He banged on the door and yelled, 'Is anybody home?'

"Granny Babe went to the door and told him to git hisself off the porch or she'd take a rolling pin to him."

"Why does that sound familiar?" whispered Papa Tom.

"Hush, honey," whispered Granny Jewel. "I want to hear what happened next."

"Mrs. Higgins stepped up behind granny, saw the panic in that young man's face and opened the door."

'Ma'am,' he said, 'I am terrified of thunder storms. Will you please let me hide under your bed until the storm's over.'

"Yes, young man, you're free to go in the front room and take shelter under the bed."

When the storm moved on, the soldier crawled out from under the bed, thanked Mrs. Higgins and left. My granny was still mad as a hornet, "How come you to do that?" she asked, arms folded across her bosom, a frown equal to a thunder cloud.

"He was nothing more than a young'un, Babe, a long way from home. It didn't matter that he was in a uniform or where he came from. Scared is scared. Someday my little son may be in the army, like his daddy. Maybe some kind person will give him shelter."

Rain could be heard gushing through the down spouts and dripping off the roof. Papa Tom broke the silence. "I'd better go downstairs and check the damage. It sounded like something exploded in the living room. All followed at a slower pace. With windows and doors closed, the house was now hot and stuffy. When they reached the front hall, James threw open the front door, inhaling the cool south breeze.

"Oh, no!" was heard from the living room. Scattered across the floor was splintered wood and glass. "A surge of electricity from the lightning came through the wiring and blew up the radio," exclaimed Papa Tom, his voice full of dismay. "What are we going to do tonight if we can't hear the news?"

"Amos and Andy are on tonight. We can't miss them," said Peggy.

"This will never do! I'm going to Morehead City as soon as possible and buy a brand new radio from Eastman's Furniture. Who'd like to help me choose one?"

"Mama, you'd better volunteer," whispered Peggy. "I'm going to clean up this mess. It's important to get every sliver of glass or bare feet will find it."

"You're right, honey. If I know your father, he'll find the biggest, most outlandish radio in the store," said Granny Jewel. In a loud voice, she replied, "I'll come with you, dear. Who knows, I may see a chair that would look perfect in here."

"Oh, no, that storm may be the most expensive one the whole summer."

As they were leaving, the telephone rang. "I'll get it," called Sarah.

"I can't believe how dedicated that child is to answering the phone," mumbled Clara, a broom in one hand and a dust pan in the other.

"Did you survive the storm?" asked Bruce.

"You won't believe where the whole family, plus a cat and dog, rode out the storm."

"I can't imagine."

Sarah laughingly told of their experience. It all seemed a bit silly now since the sun was pouring in the windows and birds had resumed their chirping.

"That black cloud and rumbling thunder was warning enough for my boss. We loaded the lawn mower and other equipment in the back of the truck, and headed home. By the time I got to the house, it was getting really bad. My mama made me sit on the sofa, away from a window or the fireplace. He paused for a moment. "I don't have to work the rest of the afternoon. Why don't we take a walk?"

"Can we go sailing?"

"If we can find enough breeze. A storm usually kills the wind."

Soon Bruce was tapping on the front door. Sarah, glad to get away from the house, was dressed in shorts and a shirt. She had traded her good sneakers for an old pair that was becoming threadbare.

"I don't think there's enough wind to push the boat, Sarah. Maybe we could sit on the dock and talk."

"Are you sure? It looks like a lovely day to be out on the water," she replied, disappointed.

"If we sail around the marsh, and this little breeze dies, we'll be bait for gnats and sand flies. They are worse than an attack of Japanese zeros. My daddy tells a story about a soldier during World War II who had guard duty on Cedar Island. When another soldier was brought to relieve him, they found him huddled on the ground. He had taken off his clothes and made a tent so he could get away from the sand flies."

"You've convinced me, Bruce. Let's find a dry spot on the dock and watch the boats go by."

Bruce slipped his hand in Sarah's as they found a place the sun had already dried. "Sarah," he said thoughtfully, "do you realize there's only four weeks left of summer? I don't know where the time has gone. Soon you'll be going back to Raleigh, and we'll have to wait another year before we can see each other."

"It always seems that way, Bruce. I wait all year to come to Beaufort, and the summer's gone before I can blink my eyes." Sarah smiled at the handsome boy sitting beside her. "My grandpapa keeps me busy most of the time at the store. I'm not complaining," she hurried to explain.

"I'll be able to buy most of my school clothes with the money I've earned. Granny Jewel got her fall Sears Roebuck catalog in the mail, and it's full of all the new fashions. I can buy whatever I like since I'll be spending my money."

"I've saved most of my money from mowing lawns, too. It helps my parents if I can buy my school clothes. Mama used to say she was going to put a brick on my head to keep me from growing so fast." Bruce smiled at Sarah and slipped his arm around her shoulder. "I can hear my mama now. 'Brucie,'" she'd say, "'you outgrow your britches before I can get them home from the store.'"

Sarah laughed. "My friends all say if I don't stop growing, I'll be a foot taller than all the boys, and nobody will ask me for a date."

"If that's the case, I hope I keep right on growing."

Sarah glanced at her watch. "It's getting close to supper time. I guess we'd better go. The slight breeze which had come up after the storm was now only a whisper, the water a mirror. Both began to rub their eyes and scratch their arms and legs.

"The sand flies found us, Sarah. We'd better go before we start inhaling them." Quickly Bruce pulled Sarah to her feet and hurried her off the dock.

"We're only half a block from my uncle's house," Sarah said as they walked toward Ann Street. "Would you like to stop in a minute? Aunt Miriam is supposed to be there putting dishes and glasses in her new kitchen cabinets. She says decorating with the wedding presents reminds her of playing with a doll house when she was little."

Stepping on the front porch, Sarah called through the screen door, "Yoo, hoo, Aunt Miriam." Sarah turned to Bruce and whispered, "I hear a strange sound in the back of the house. It sounds like someone *crying*!"

"Maybe the house is haunted," suggested Bruce. "It could be the spirit of a young girl who was carried off by sand flies."

"Bruce! This is serious! I know the sound of someone crying, after all, I have a younger brother *and* sister. I'm afraid something terrible has happened to Aunt Miriam!"

At this, Bruce pushed open the door and entered the spacious hall, Sarah close behind.

"Mrs. Mitchell," he called in a deep voice, "Are you all right?"

Their sneakers made squeaky noises on the wooden floors as Sarah and Bruce hurried toward the sound of someone weeping. Both stopped in the kitchen doorway when they saw Miriam Mitchell sitting cross-legged in the middle of the kitchen floor, surrounded by water. She turned her tear stained face toward the couple. Between sobs, she managed, "I give up! Herb was right! Fixing up this old house has been a nightmare. Nothing has gone right!" She struggled to her feet, dripping water. "I decided to come by after the storm to unpack more boxes. As soon as I opened the front door I could hear water dripping. When I got to the kitchen, water was pouring down the side of the wall and into the new kitchen cabinets. The bedroom over the kitchen is ruined, too. The new paint and plaster is already cracked and peeling off."

Sarah gathered her aunt in her arms, trying to think of comforting words.

"The roof has new shingles. Why would it leak?" implored Miriam.

"I'm going in the attic and find out what happened," announced Bruce. He disappeared up the stairs, two steps at a time.

"Aunt Miriam," said Sarah, in a take-charge voice very much like her grandmother's, "I'm going to sweep this water out the back door. With the windows and doors open, the linoleum floor should dry in no time."

"The floor is not the worst part, Sarah. The rain poured in my new kitchen cabinets, soaking the new dishes. Everything will have to be taken out and washed again. We'll never be out of the apartment in *two days*!"

"Please don't fret. I promise everything will be ready on moving day. You're exhausted, so everything seems worse than it really is." Sarah reached to open a cabinet door. "Why, we'll take some clean towels and dry up all the water, and everything will be good as new."

Before Sarah opened the door, she noticed a thin stream of water dripping on the counter. Before Miriam could warn her, Sarah threw open the door, and was met by a rush of cold water splashing in her face and running down the front of her shirt. Shocked, Sarah turned to her aunt and started to speak. Instead, laughter burst from her throat. Sarah immediately clapped her hands over her mouth. "I'm sorry, Aunt Miriam! It's not funny. I didn't mean to laugh." A giggle escaped before she could contain it. To her surprise, her aunt smiled back.

"Sarah, we are a sorry sight! Anyone would think we had been in swimming, only we aren't covered in salt water."

"And we won't have to shower tonight. We've already had our bath." This remark set off another round of giggles.

Bruce returned from the attic, anxious to tell the problem was an attic window that had been left open. Once more he stopped at the kitchen door, wonder written on his face. Before he could ask what was happening, he heard the front door open. "Hello," called a deep voice. Bruce hurried toward the front of the house.

"Hello, Mr. Mitchell."

"Well, Bruce, is Sarah here, and have you seen my wife?"

"Yes, sir, Sarah's here. She's in the kitchen with Mrs. Mitchell."

"Is anything wrong? You look worried."

"Uh, no sir, everything's OK, I guess," replied Bruce, shaking his head slowly. "The storm flooded your house, ruining the paint and plaster, upstairs and down. It got in the new kitchen cabinets, and messed up all the dishes. Mrs. Mitchell and Sarah are sitting in the kitchen floor, soaking wet crying and laughing their heads off." Bruce thought a minute. "Other than that, I guess everything's all right."

Sarah worked the following day so her uncle could repair the damage done by the storm. While sipping a cup of hot coffee early that morning, Herb Mitchell felt sick thinking about the condition of the house and new furniture being delivered the following morning. The apartment had to be vacated by late that afternoon. As he turned onto Moore Street from Ann Street, he looked at the freshly painted front porch. It was filled with teens, armed with buckets, brooms, brushes, and towels. When they spotted him, one called, "Good morning, Mr. Mitchell. We're here to help."

Herb Mitchell stopped at the bottom step, mouth open. "I, I don't understand. Where did you kids come from?"

Nancy Russert, dressed in starched shorts and shirt, replied, "Sarah called last night and told me what happened. I called John, and we called practically everyone in Mrs. Mitchell's English classes." She smiled at the students behind her. "We all want to help."

"Why?"

A boy from the back of the group stepped forward. "Mrs. Mitchell is the best teacher we ever had. She really cares about her students, and we care about her." All nodded.

"Welcome everyone." said Herb, with outstretched arms. "You're an answer to prayer."

With windows and doors open, a fresh breeze from the ocean filled the house with cool air. The girls tackled the kitchen, washing dishes that were still sitting in rain water, and relining shelves with paper. Upstairs, the guys were scraping, patching and repainting the damaged walls. By mid morning, a soft "Yoo, hoo," was heard. Miss

Nettie Blackwell stepped inside, armed with freshly baked chocolate chip cookies, a frosted pitcher of lemonade and a stack of paper cups.

"You're a life saver, Miss Nettie," declared Herb Mitchell.

The only chair in the house was brought hastily to the living room for the older guest. While the group gratefully munched warm cookies and drank the icy lemonade, Miss Nettie entertained the teens with stories of their parents when they were her students.

At noon, Miriam Mitchell opened the front door, wonder written on her face. "Herb," she called, setting a cardboard box on the floor, "what's happening?"

"Surprise!" shouted the teens, stopping work to greet their beloved teacher. Guided by the girls, Miriam was escorted to the now sparkling kitchen. The cabinet doors were opened, revealing freshly scrubbed, shiny dishes and glasses. To their dismay, the teacher burst into tears. The students, all crowded in the tiny room fell silent.

"Did we do it wrong?" Nancy asked timidly.

"No, my dears! Everything is perfect! And to think it was done by the people I love so much!"

By five o'clock, Bruce came by on his way to Mitchell's Grocery. Herb was sitting on the front steps resting. "I heard what happened today, Mr. Mitchell," he said, sitting down. "Billy Stanley told me Mrs. Mitchell cried when she saw the kitchen all fixed up."

"That's right, Bruce."

"But, Mr. Mitchell, she cried when the kitchen was flooded. Why did she cry when it was dry?"

"I don't know, Bruce." He looked off in the distance and shook his head. "We may never know."

Chapter 13

"Look, Daddy, look!" demanded Amy, bending over her grandmother's flower bed. "The flowers aren't thirsty any more 'cause the rain gave them a drink of water."

James shoved his heavy suitcase across the seat of his pick up truck and turned to inspect the flowers. "All they needed was a good soaking, and brother, they got it."

Both looked as the front screen door closed. Peggy stepped on the porch, wearing a sorrowful expression. "Honey," she began, "do you have to go? The plant has gotten along fine without you for a month."

"Peggy, I've called Malcolm Vane, the plant supervisor, every day to make sure everything is going smoothly. Still, I feel like I need to get back and see for myself. Besides, our telephone bill is going to be sky high."

"Herb and Miriam want us to eat supper with them tomorrow night in their new home. It will be a celebration."

"You're not making this any easier for me but I feel I can't wait another day." James Bowers smiled at his pretty wife. "If I stay any longer, I'll gain fifty pounds. You know I have to have second helpings on all Clara's cooking." After a tearful farewell, James climbed into his truck and headed west down Ann Street, and over the Beaufort bridge.

Peggy turned in time to see her parents coming out of the house. "Where are you going?" she asked.

"We're on a mission, dear," said her mother, winking broadly.

"Yes, honey, when the news comes on tonight, we'll be able to hear it loud and clear. There may be a radio at Eastman's Furniture powerful enough to pick up WPTF in Raleigh."

"That would have to be a mighty big radio, Daddy."

"We have a mighty big living room. It can hold it."

Granny Jewel stood apart, vigorously shaking her head.

I probably should go along, thought Peggy. *Someone is going to need to referee that pair. Let me see, it will be a huge, dark, thunderous cabinet, or a small radio that matches the furniture.* Peggy shook her head and smiled. The outcome would be interesting.

Peggy stepped into the cool hall as the phone rang. "Good morning to you, too, Bruce." She paused, listening. "Yes, thank you, we're all well. I'll call Sarah."

"Hi, Bruce," Sarah said brightly, holding the phone close to her ear. "Do you think there's enough wind? Sure I'd love to go!" Sarah replaced the receiver with a bang.

"Mama!"

"I'm in the dining room."

"Bruce wants to take me sailing." A worried looked crossed the mother's pretty face. "Don't worry. I'll remember to duck when we're 'coming about.'"

A fresh breeze off the ocean with an incoming tide made tacking necessary. Sarah was fascinated as the wooden hull effortlessly cut through the clear, sea-green water.

"When we get out in the inlet, I'll let you take the tiller," said Bruce. "You'll love sailing even more when you're at the helm." He glanced at the pretty girl beside him. "Someday," he said, running his hand lovingly along the gunwale, "I'll find a girl I love almost as much as 'Willa', and when I do, I'll ask her to marry me."

"Hmmm," murmured Sarah, trailing a hand in the cool water, "Willa would be stiff competition for any girl."

Bruce's smile faded. He placed his arm, brown from the summer sun, around Sarah's shoulder. "No, Sarah. I *already* think about you more than I do Willa. Usually by this time, I've hauled her up, scraped the barnacles off her bottom, and given her a fresh coat of white paint. I've been real neglectful this summer."

"At least you won't have to worry about that with a real girl," added Sarah, their laughter blending.

Sarah watched as Bruce busied himself with the sail. She liked Bruce, really liked him. She met other boys during the summer at church or at the grocery store, but had not felt attracted to any of them. *What if,* she thought, gazing at towering cumulus clouds on the horizon, *what if Bruce and I date every summer, and someday fall in love. After college, we could get married at St. Paul's, and he could teach school. I could, well . . . I could do whatever it is I'm going to do. We could have two kids and go sailing every Sunday afternoon.*

Sarah's daydream was suddenly interrupted. "Did you see that?" cried Bruce. The girl sat up quickly, scanning the rolling waves of the inlet. "What was it?"

"A bluefish jumped out of the water ahead of the boat. He must have been sixteen inches long!" Bruce dove for a wooden box wedged under the forward seat. Prying off the lid, he pulled out a ball of twine.

"What are you going to do, try to lasso him?"

"No, my girl, I'm going to hook him!"

From the box, Bruce produced a small paper bag of hooks attached to long white pieces if bone. He quickly tied a length of twine to the bone and tossed it over the stern.

"Don't you need to bait the hook? My grandfather always uses shrimp or fiddler crabs to catch fish."

"The loon bone is my lure," managed Bruce, now fiercely intent on tying the line to the boat.

"I don't understand!"

With everything set, the boy had more time to explain. "If you're trolling, the white loon bone will look like a minnow. The fish bites, and he's hooked!"

"Why do you call it a loon bone?"

"You know the beautiful black and white bird you see swimming and diving in the inlet?" Sarah nodded. "Lures are made from their leg bones."

"Oh, the poor birds!"

Bruce laughed. "Don't worry, Sarah. We don't take the bone until the rest of him is stewing in a pot, along with taters and onions."

"That seems so cruel," said Sarah, angrily.

"It's not cruel if a man has to feed his family and doesn't have a job, like during the Depression. My granddaddy used to tell us there were no jobs anywhere. Without gardens and food from the sea, people would have starved."

"What about giant sea turtles we see coming up for air? Surely people don't kill them!" Sarah searched her boyfriend's face.

Before Bruce could answer, he felt a sharp tug on the line. "Here, Sarah, bring him in! The tugging and jerking on the line caused the girl to forget the fate of turtles and loons.

By four o'clock, the boat was clean, sails furled and a bucket of fat, silver fish had been cleaned. Sarah and neighborhood cats watched as

Bruce expertly scaled and cleaned the catch of the day. When finished, Bruce and Sarah walked the few blocks to Granny Jewel's house. They walked slowly, trying to stretch a perfect day.

"I'm glad you're my girl, Sarah," said Bruce, glancing sidelong at the girl beside him. "I don't know what I'll do this winter while you're gone."

"I know, Bruce. I wish I lived here all year."

At the front steps, Bruce squeezed her hand. "I'll call you tomorrow."

"That would be great, Bruce."

Sarah stepped inside the house and headed for the kitchen. Granny Jewel was setting the table and Peggy was washing Amy's hands outside at the garden hose. "Your little sister has been baking this afternoon," said the grandmother. "There are mud pies and cakes drying on the back porch."

Sarah smiled. "That's nice. I know Clara will be relieved to have someone help her with the cooking."

"How did you like sailing out of Taylor's Creek?" asked Papa Tom, passing a bowl of vegetables.

"It's so pretty, Papa Tom! Outside the inlet is the Atlantic Ocean. I strained my eyes, but I couldn't see Portugal. We got busy catching fish, so I didn't notice anything else but getting those fish in the boat."

"Papa Tom," wailed Joshua, "make her take me next time. I want to go fishing in the inlet."

Sarah smiled at her brother. "I promise, Joshua. The next time we go, you can come, too. I'll ask Bruce tomorrow if" . . . Before Sarah could finish her sentence, she was interrupted by the ringing of the telephone.

"I'll get it," offered Clara. "You folks finish your supper. It's probably that boy Sarah makes goo-goo eyes at." Clara gave a disapproving sniff and headed for the hall.

"What do you mean, 'a long distance call for Sarah Bowers?' That chile don't know nobody as 'far away as Ohio. There must be some mistake."

In the dining room, the wooden silence was shattered by the clatter of silver ware being dropped on a china plate, and a chair being scraped across the wooden floor. "I do, I do, Clara! I do know somebody in Ohio." Sarah grabbed the receiver before Clara could send it crashing back in its cradle. "Hello, hello!" Sarah paused, fearful the connection was broken.

Finally, amid crackling and buzzing, Sarah heard a faint, but familiar voice. It was a voice from a summer distant, a time when they were children, but not *really* children. It was a voice she thought she had forgotten.

"Hello, Sarah? This is Porter Mason. Remember me?"

Remember you, thought Sarah, fleetingly, her mind racing. *Memories of you come when I least expect them, crowding other thoughts from my mind.*

"Yes, Porter. I remember you. You sound the same as you did three summers ago."

"Oh, has it been that long? Say, you're not married are you?" Porter gave a nervous laugh.

Sarah grinned, "No, silly. Of course I'm not married."

"Good, because my parents and I are coming to Beaufort for vacation. They want to see some of the people they met during the war. And Sarah," his voice dropped to a whisper, "I want to see you."

Sarah's mouth was suddenly dry as cotton. It was difficult to speak. "When are you coming?" she croaked.

"We're leaving in the morning and we'll drive all day. We should be in Beaufort by dark the day after tomorrow."

There followed a dreadful silence. Sarah's mind was numb. A telephone call all the way from Ohio, and she couldn't think of a thing to say!

Finally; Porter spoke. "Uh, I'd better hang up. Sarah, I'm real glad you're not in Raleigh this summer. Gotta' go. See you in two days!"

Sarah stared at the receiver then slowly lowered it. She retraced her steps as in a trance, pausing at the dining room door. All looked expectantly, waiting for an explanation.

"Who was that on the telephone, honey?" asked her mother casually.

Sarah, dazed, heard herself speak. "It was Porter Mason, Mama. You remember him, don't you?"

Before Peggy could reply, a voice from the kitchen interrupted, "Ask me if I remember that red-haired boy. You bet I do! He's the one almost got you drowned."

"Yes, Sarah, I remember Porter. One summer during the war, his mother and I became good friends. Our husbands were away serving in the military."

Clara's voice rang from the kitchen. "It was on account of him you and your grandpa were out gallivanting around the town during a killer hurricane."

Sarah slowly returned to her chair. Sitting, she stared at food which minutes before, was incredibly delicious. Now it seemed impossible to swallow even a tiny bite.

"Sarah," her grandmother whispered, "Your supper's getting cold. Fried seafood is best eaten hot."

"Yes, Ma'am," replied the girl, gently moving the food around with her fork.

"Clean your plate, Sarah," commanded her little sister. "You can't have pie if you don't clean your plate."

"Yes, Miss Amy," she answered, grateful to be spared a large slice of lemon pie.

Supper over, Sarah cleared the table then hurried to her tiny room behind the kitchen. For a time she sat in front of her vanity mirror. *My hair is a mess, my summer clothes tired and limp from so many washings. I'm a mess, a hopeless mess!* A tap on the door interrupted her thoughts. "Who is it?"

"It's your mama."

"Come in." Slowly the door opened. Peggy stepped over to the bed, eyes meeting in the mirror.

"Mama," Sarah whispered, eyes wide. "What am I going to do? My hair is a mess, and my clothes are horrible."

"The weather's hot, so you can wear your hair up."

"Suppose Porter doesn't like it that way."

"Oh, he'll like it. You look five years older. Your daddy and I are the ones who want you to look young." She smiled wistfully.

"How about my clothes, Mama? I can't let Porter see me in these awful rags."

The mother looked down, hiding a smile. "I don't understand, honey. You haven't complained all summer about your clothes."

"This is different, Mama."

"How?"

Sarah's eyes once more focused on her image in the mirror. "I don't know. I just know it is."

Peggy stood and smoothed the bedspread. "Well, my lovely girl, there is nothing to do but go shopping." Sarah gave her mother a quizzical look. "Oh, yes, Sarah. Ever since Eve tried on different fig leaves to find the one she liked best, women have shopped for all sorts of reasons. It could be for fun, or if they're feeling blue, or out of necessity. In your case, it's necessity." Peggy walked to the door and paused. "We'll start first thing in the morning. I'll ask your grandmother to keep Amy so we can concentrate. We don't need her hiding under racks of dresses and talking to mannequins while you are making up your mind."

"Oh, yes! That will be fun!"

Peggy winked. "It's a mother's responsibility to train her daughter in the fine art of shopping."

"Are you going to listen to the evening news with Papa Tom?"

Peggy nodded her head slowly. "We should be able to pick it up with no static tonight. That gigantic floor model looks more like a coffin than a radio."

"How does Granny Jewel like it?"

"She pretends it's not there."

Sarah thought about the huge, dark cabinet sitting in the living room, the insides filled with large silver tubes glowing a ghostly green light. It had taken Papa Tom and Uncle Herb to get it in the house.

Peggy grinned. "It looks like daddy won a round, at last."

"I could hardly sleep last night," said Sarah as she and Peggy hurried toward Front Street. It was barely nine o'clock, the sun already hot, promising another scorching day. Shore birds could be heard on the outer islands, their faint cries borne on the cool south breeze.

"You deserve new clothes, honey. You've spent most of your summer working in your grandfather's store, you helped paint your uncle's house, and you've helped me with Amy. You deserve a whole new wardrobe."

"I've been looking at pretty clothes in the store windows all summer. I didn't want to buy any, because I've been saving my money for school clothes. Now, suddenly, it's important to have something new and pretty."

"Those outfits may be on sale now, since summer is nearly over."

"They may be sold already," added Sarah sadly.

Peggy changed the subject. "Sarah, how long has it been since you saw Porter?"

"It was the summer I was thirteen."

"Porter is old enough to go to college. He's not going to be the boy you knew. He's a young man."

Sarah slowed her step. "Mama, he sounded the same on the telephone." She glanced up, staring at the bough of a spreading elm. "You know, I believe his voice was deeper. Mama, I wonder if I sounded different."

"You've grown into a lovely young woman in the past three years, Sarah."

"That's one reason I want to look my best. I'm not a little girl anymore"

Laden with packages, the two stepped inside the cool house as the family was sitting down to lunch. "Your trip must have been successful," said Granny Jewel, her eyes resting on brightly colored boxes and bags. "It looks like you bought out the stores."

"We had to go to several places, Granny Jewel, to match shorts and tops," said Sarah, hurrying to wash up and join the others.

"I never realized how much strength it takes to go shopping," said Sarah, between bites of shrimp salad. "I'm tired!"

"Oh, yes," said Papa Tom. "It takes years of concentration and physical conditioning to be a shopper." He winked at his granddaughter. "Your grandmother has been in training all her life and, I might add, she is a champion."

Choosing to ignore her husband, the grandmother suggested, "Why don't you call Nancy and see if she is free this afternoon. You could drive to Morehead City and look for summer clothes."

"Dear," interrupted Papa Tom, "I would imagine Sarah is too weary to do any more shopping today."

"Oh, no, Papa Tom," Sarah cried. "I'm not *really* tired. In fact, I'm bursting with energy! I'll call Nancy after lunch and see if she's free." Sarah wore a troubled expression. "If she's practicing, she won't go. She doesn't let anything interfere with piano."

Luckily, Nancy had practiced for several hours that morning. "I'd love to go shopping, Sarah! I need new school clothes."

Car windows down, radio blaring, the girls drove across the causeway connecting the two towns. North of the narrow ribbon of road, vast reaches of salt marsh stretched almost to the channel which led to the Intracoastal Waterway. Today the girls were too busy to appreciate the azure sky, and sparkling blue-green salt water.

"Nancy," began Sarah, gripping the steering wheel of her family's Pontiac sedan. "Do you remember a boy named Porter Mason? He was here three summers ago."

"Oh, yes," replied Nancy hurriedly. "Who could forget him?" She was thoughtful for a moment. "I remember he was here during the war with his mother."

"Yeah. I met him the summer we were twelve."

"You have a good memory, Sarah."

I remember it like it was yesterday, thought Sarah.

"What about him?"

"He's coming for a visit."

"Wow! If I remember correctly, he was cute as pie. Hmmm, didn't he have dark red hair?" She gave Sarah a sidelong glance. "I'll bet he's cuter than ever."

Sarah stared straight ahead as the car rumbled across the Morehead City bridge. She could feel her fingers gripping the steering wheel tighter than necessary.

"Where is he from?"

"Canton, Ohio."

Nancy gave Sarah her full attention. "How do you know he's coming to Beaufort?"

Sarah inhaled deeply and smiled at her friend. "Because he called me *long distance*! He wanted to make sure I was here, not in Raleigh."

"Wow!" breathed Nancy, looking at her friend with new respect.

Downtown, the girls rode in silence searching for a parking place. Before they could get out of the car, Nancy turned. "Sarah, what about Bruce? You all are going steady. You're wearing his rhinestone necklace." Her voice sounded accusing.

"I think he'll understand, Nancy. Porter and I are friends, old friends."

"I don't think he'll fall for that 'old friends' idea."

"Oh, Nancy," snapped Sarah, wiping beads of perspiration from her upper lip. "Let's get out of this car before we bake alive."

The cool interior of the Fashion Center was a relief from the heat. The girls noticed that the stores in Morehead City were now displaying their fall line. Dresses and suits in brown, gold and green wool or gabardine were artfully displayed on mannequins or hung on racks. Dazzling costume jewelry, scarves and matching gloves arrayed counter tops.

"Isn't it exciting to see new clothes for the fall and winter?" whispered Nancy. "I'm ready to dump my old, tired summer clothes."

Sarah shook her head. "I'm not thinking about fall clothes yet. I'll shop in Raleigh for them. I'm still interested in summer clothes."

"May I help you, ladies?" asked a friendly clerk. Before they could reply, "You must be shopping for back to school clothes."

"No, Ma'am," answered Sarah. "I'm interested in summer things."

"All of our summer clothes are on sale at the back of the store. There may still be a few things in your size." The clerk sounded doubtful.

"Oooh, look, Nancy! Two sun back dresses in my size. One is flowered cotton, the other white eyelet embroidery."

"The white dress looks great with your tan," commented Nancy when Sarah stepped out of the dressing room.

"You must mean my grocery store tan. I haven't had time to lie on the beach and take a sun bath," said Sarah, returning to the dressing room. Soon she emerged, wearing the dress with bold, splashy colors of green, blue and lavender.

"Oh, that dress is gorgeous with your dark hair. There's no way to choose, so you'll have to buy both."

Sarah looked troubled. "I don't have enough money for both. The money I saved from working this summer is for fall clothes."

"I have an idea!" squealed Nancy, jumping off the stool where she had been sitting. "You buy one, and I'll buy one! After we have worn them, we can trade."

"What a great idea!" exclaimed Sarah. "Try them on and make sure they fit."

When the girls returned, Sarah kept the white dress, determined to wear it the first night she saw Porter.

The following day, time seemed to stand still. When the soft gray of dawn showed in Sarah's tiny window, she was already staring at the ceiling. She heard Mr. Peavy tune up and announce the beginning of a new day. I'll see Porter *today*, she kept telling herself. Still, it didn't seem possible. As she dressed in shorts and shirt, Sarah imagined herself seated on the front porch in the cool of the evening, engrossed in a book, when he stepped on the porch. *I shall be wearing my best Sunday dress and sandals polished white as snow. I'll be friendly, but not too friendly, and invite him to sit in one of Granny Jewel's rocking chairs banked in soft, fluffy pillows. I'll ask him questions about the trip, his parents, and college plans. I'll think of witty, intelligent things to say that will make him laugh. I might even flirt . . .*

"Sarah, your breakfast is going to be stone cold if you don't stop dragging your feet and get out here." Clara's voice was laced with irritation.

"I'm coming, Clara," the girl called. Forgotten were thoughts of the front porch at twilight.

After breakfast, Sarah carefully ironed her new clothes and hung them in her tiny closet. She made her bed and dusted the furniture. "Clara," she asked, emerging from her room, "would you like me to dust and vacuum the living room?"

"Clara never did turn down an offer like that. Help yourself." The woman glanced sideways, squinting one eye. "You wouldn't be sprucin' up the house on account of that boy, would you?"

"Oh, no, Clara. I just want to help." Sarah paused. "Actually, it is why I'm doing it. He's coming tonight and I want everything perfect."

"Clean to your heart's content, honey."

By noon, Sarah had vacuumed, polished and dusted every surface downstairs. Peggy walked in the living room as Sarah was winding the vacuum cord. "Mama," she wailed, "I've done everything I can think of, and it's only lunchtime! This day will never end!" She gave the machine a mighty yank and headed for the storage closet.

"Hmmm, I think the living room could use a bouquet of fresh flowers, don't you? Why don't you run down to Beaufort Florist and have one of the ladies make a low arrangement for the coffee table."

Sarah brightened. "That's a great idea, Mama. Only, don't we have a few flowers blooming in the back yard?"

"No, dear," answered Granny Jewel, stepping into the room. "The drought killed the flowers in the backyard."

Mother and daughter watched as Sarah hurried from the house, letting the front door slam behind her. "Mama, I'm sure we could find enough flowers in the yard for one bouquet."

"Yes, my dear, but, Sarah is impatient." She placed her arm lovingly around her daughter. "Surely you can remember how slowly the hands of the clock move when you're going to see the person you love."

"Love?" asked Peggy, looking at her mother. "Sarah's never said a word about loving Porter."

Granny Jewel slowly shook her head. "She doesn't have to."

Chapter 14

After supper, Papa Tom settled in his favorite chair before the monster radio. Carefully turning the wooden dial, he stopped the glowing needle on a station broadcasting world news. Granny Jewel sat across the room, pretending indifference toward the offending, wooden presence crouching in her living room.

Sarah, her hair in bobby pins, saw a chance for a long, hot soak in the bath tub. "Mama, if Bruce calls, tell him I . . ., uh . . ., I'm . . ."

"How about, in the bath tub," added her mother.

"Yes, but I don't want him coming around tonight," she hissed.

"Sarah, *you'll* have to tell him." Her mother's expression tightened.

Looking troubled, Sarah replied, "This is getting complicated, Mama."

"Bruce called yesterday, and you used shopping as an excuse for not seeing him. Today he called, and you told him you had to clean house. What will be your excuse if he calls tonight?" Peggy, impatient, placed her hands on her hips.

"That's easy." Sarah smiled. "I'll tell him we have company from Ohio. It's not a lie." Sarah looked troubled. "It's not *really* a lie."

"It sure puts a strain on the truth."

Sarah finished dressing and was painting her fingernails a soft pink when the telephone rang. No one moved to answer it. *Oh, well,* the girl decided, *I've got to do this. She walked toward the hall, blowing on the wet polish.*

"Hello, Bruce . . . . Yes, I know we've both been busy . . . . Tonight? Well, we're expecting company from Ohio any minute. It's a family we met years ago." There was a long pause. All sound from the living room had ceased. "Only one child . . . A son. How old is he? Gee, I'm not sure. Bruce," she said quickly, "I have to go. I think Mama needs me to tuck Amy in."

Quietly, Sarah placed the receiver in its cradle. A thick silence followed. She took a step, then another. Peering around the door facing, she locked eyes with her grandfather.

"Sarah," he asked quietly, "what kind of game are you playing?"

"I'm not playing a game," she snapped defensively. "I didn't lie. I don't know Porter's *exact* age, because I don't remember his birthday."

"Maybe you didn't tell an out-and-out lie, but you sure bent the truth."

Sarah moved across the room and sat on the corner of the sofa. "I'm not hurting anybody, Papa."

"Yes, you are, Sarah. You're hurting yourself."

Sarah could feel her eyes begin to sting. Before tears could spill, she stood and moved toward the front door. "I'm going to sit on the porch. Porter could be here any time."

At nine o'clock, the last trace of daylight was gone. Night descended, street lamps winked on. "She's going to be carried away by mosquitoes," whispered Granny Jewel during a commercial for Royal pudding.

"Even if I thought she might need a blood transfusion, I wouldn't call her in," retorted the grandfather.

"Isn't that a little harsh?"

"No more harsh than the lesson she's going to learn if she keeps up this foolishness."

At ten o'clock, the family started moving toward the stairs. Papa Tom checked to make sure the back door was closed. The monster in the living room was silent, its glowing tubes dark.

Sarah, from her vantage point, watched each car pass, thinking one would soon stop. Peggy opened the screen door several inches. "Honey, we're going to bed. Are you coming?"

"I'm not sleepy, Mama. I want to stay up a little longer." She swatted a mosquito on her arm. "Maybe I'll come in and read."

With family settled upstairs, the house became like a tomb. Only one small lamp was left burning. An occasional creaking noise and the hum of an occasional car passing punctuated the silence. Soft cushions, and the absence of biting insects, had a soothing effect on the weary girl. Soon, she began to nod. Long hours and strenuous activities of the day conspired against her. Sarah sank into deep, untroubled sleep.

A footfall on the porch some time later did nothing to rouse the girl. A young man, glancing in the living room window, smiled slowly. The girl he had traveled two days to be with was curled on the sofa, asleep. He leaned forward, studying her features intently. Curly dark hair framed her oval face. Full, expressive lips parted slightly as she breathed. *She's more beautiful than I remember,* he thought.

Softly, so as not to rouse the family, he gave the familiar *rat-a tat-tat, rat-a tat-tat* on the screen door frame. Coming awake, Sarah thought for a minute she was twelve again, and her pal, Porter, was at the door.

Eyes blinking, she muttered, "No, I'm not twelve and I didn't dream the special knock. She hastily smoothed her hair, brushed wrinkles from her dress and hurried toward the front door. Her first impression was one of surprise. Porter filled the doorway far more than he had in the past. She slowly opened the door wide enough for the tall, handsome young man to enter.

"You're taller," were her first words.

"You are, too," he replied.

Standing awkwardly in the front hall, Sarah was overcome with the desire to giggle. When Porter laughed softly, she could hold her laughter no longer. A hand over her mouth made her want to laugh all the more.

"Come in and sit down," she invited.

"Maybe I'd better. At this rate, we'll wake up the whole family," Porter whispered.

"Not a chance. My mother and grandparents sleep like the dead. Nothing wakes them."

Overhead, the grandmother sat up in bed. "Thomas," she whispered, "I think Sarah's guest has arrived."

"It sounds like it. That boy has driven two days and came calling at midnight. He must be mighty smitten with our girl."

"It makes me feel old."

"Try to get some sleep, my love. I think we're going to need our strength."

Downstairs, the young couple sat across from each other, suddenly self conscious.

Sarah, studying a button on the front of her dress, asked, "Uh, how was your trip?"

Relieved, the boy launched into a detailed account of long, hot hours on the highway, a flat tire somewhere in Pennsylvania and a few wrong turns.

When finished, he asked, "What have you been doing this summer besides swimming, boating and fishing?"

"None of the above," Sarah answered. "I worked in my grandfather's grocery store weekdays and helped around the house when needed." She saw this response brought an admiring expression. "But," she added with haste, "I don't have to work this week, or the rest of the summer."

"Did he fire you?"

"No, silly," laughed Sarah, noting his grin. One thing about Porter had not changed. He still loved to tease.

"I'd better go and let you get some sleep." He yawned and stretched. "I'm feeling a little tired myself."

"Aren't you afraid you'll wake up your parents?"

"We have two rooms at the Inlet Inn. I can't sleep on a cot at the foot of their bed any longer. I'd hang off both ends."

At the door he turned. "How about tomorrow? On the trip, when I wasn't thinking about you, I thought about that cool, clear water in Taylor's Creek. Would you like to go swimming in the morning?" He smiled at the girl. "I need to get started on my sun tan. I can't go back as pale as when I left."

Sarah returned his smile. "You have to be careful. We can't have people mistaking you for a lobster."

His expression grew serious. "Are you *sure* you don't have other plans."

Fleetingly, Sarah thought of the boy with whom all summer she had shared happy, tender moments. She thought of the rhinestone necklace worn with pride that now lay in her jewelry box. "No, I'm free." At that moment she would have cancelled plans with the president. Gently, Porter cupped her face with both hands, brought his face close and brushed his lips against hers. Sarah, eyes closed, felt a tingle down to her toes.

When he was gone, she quietly closed the front door and leaned against it. Finally, turning out the living room lamp, she glided toward the back of the house, one finger on her lips. *I don't tingle when Bruce kisses me. What can be the difference?*

Before Sarah could eat a bite of Clara's fluffy, pale yellow scrambled eggs, the familiar *rat-a-tat-tat, rat-a-tat-tat,* was heard. She dropped her fork, slid back the chair and was almost in the hall before anyone at the table could look up.

"My goodness, our girl is spry this morning!" exclaimed Papa Tom.

"Love causes a person to do extraordinary things," remarked the grandmother between sips of steamy hot coffee.

Sarah, returning, wore a dazzling expression. "You all remember Porter, don't you?"

Papa Tom stood and offered an outstretched hand as the family greeted the young man. "It's nice to see all of you again," Porter remarked politely.

"Won't you join us?" asked Peggy Bowers. Porter remembered Sarah telling him that, in the south, people were always invited for a meal, but it was not polite to accept on short notice. However, the odors coming from the kitchen made his knees weak.

"No, thank you, Mrs. Bowers. I'm fine."

Clara appeared in the doorway, a plate heaped with scrambled eggs, bacon, hot biscuits and stewed apples in her hand. "That's a mighty hollow sounding voice to me," she said, shoving Sarah's plate over. "Get this boy some silver, honey." She looked the young man up and down. "Humph, filling out a frame like that is going to take a lot of serious cooking."

Porter appeared genuinely happy to see her. "Hello, Clara. Remember me?"

"How could I forget you? You keep showing up. Coffee, or milk?" Clara asked.

"Is it the same kind of milk you had a few summers ago?"

"We've been drinking Mrs. Carraway's milk for forty years. I guess we'll keep on until the cows run dry," said Papa Tom, smiling.

"In Canton, the big dairy farms are homogenizing and pasteurizing milk."

"What does *that* mean?" asked Joshua, grimacing.

"It removes any bacteria from the milk," answered Porter, between bites.

"Who's going to tell Mrs. Carraway her milk has bacteria swimming around in it?" asked Sarah.

Porter, changing the subject, asked, "May I borrow Sarah this morning? I can hardly wait to go swimming in Taylor's Creek."

"Why don't you kids take the boat and row across the channel? It will be more peaceful than swimming in front of the Inlet Inn. That shore is always full of young kids and their mamas."

"That's swell, Mr. Mitchell," said their guest between bites of crisp brown bacon and fluffy scrambled eggs.

"I'll fix a picnic lunch in case we're not back at noon."

"I'll make sandwiches for you two, if you promise to stay out of my kitchen," bargained Clara.

"Fine. I'll put on my bathing suit, and be ready to go."

Armed with oars, oarlocks and a huge picnic basket, the two headed for Front Street and Papa Tom's small, wooden skiff. "I want to see Capt. Jake, Sarah. I learned a lot about boats from him when I was here."

"Morgan Stewart asks about you. Do you remember him? He and Mary adopted a war orphan. She's Amy's age." Sarah tried to think of other information about the people of Beaufort that might interest her friend.

"Mr. Sterwart was sitting on his porch this morning. When he saw me he said, "Why if it isn't the boy from Ohio!"" He grinned at the girl beside him. "He asked if I had come all that distance to court Tom Mitchell's beautiful granddaughter."

"And what did you tell him?"

"Oh," he said, shifting the weight of the wooden oars, "I told him I was going to try my very best."

"What did Mr. Stewart say?"

"He laughed and slapped his knee. I didn't stay long because I was anxious to see you." Porter grinned at Sarah from under the brim of his hat.

When they stepped on the dock, Porter spied the small white rowboat. "I thought you grandfather's boat was bigger."

"It's the same boat. You're bigger."

Porter grinned and winked. "That's OK. It's just right for two."

With the lunch and beach towels stowed, Sarah untied the bow line while Porter adjusted the oarlocks and oars. Soon, the graceful boat was skimming out toward the middle of the channel. Sarah sat in the bow and watched the shoreline recede. It was a relief to see the docks and buildings slip away and be alone with Porter. The slapping of waves on the side of the boat, and shore birds overhead were their only companions.

When they neared the opposite shore, Sarah made a suggestion. "Let's anchor out a few feet because the tide is falling. We don't want the boat to be high and dry when we start home.

Porter shipped the oars and Sarah threw the anchor overboard. "If we can't float the boat off, we'll have to stay here all night." He looked across the channel. "We could stretch out on our towels and count the stars when it got dark. Tomorrow morning, when the tide is high, we could row back."

"My grandpapa would never allow such a thing. He'd be over here in a matter of seconds before dark."

"Ah, you forget. We have his boat!"

Sarah, wading ashore with the picnic basket turned. "Papa Tom has been swimming Taylor's Creek since he was Joshua's age. He could be over here in a matter of minutes."

"You can't blame a guy for trying," he said, taking the basket. Porter put the picnic basket on the white sand above the tide line. Now," he announced, "it's time to go swimming!" He threw his hat and shirt on the towel, let out a war whoop and headed for the cool water of Taylor's Creek. He dove under and surfaced several feet away. "Come on, Sarah, the water's great!"

Sarah, wearing the new bathing suit bought the day before in Morehead City, followed more slowly. Porter disappeared once more, surfacing near her. "You look different with your hair wet and plastered against your head," she said, laughing.

"No different than you're going to look." He dove under, grabbed the girl's ankles, and gave a jerk. Sarah squealed as she was pulled under. With her eyes open, she saw Porter's face close to hers. Suddenly, before they surfaced, he kissed her. Both came up laughing and gasping for air. "That was my first underwater kiss," admitted Porter.

"Mine, too," confessed Sarah.

When tired of swimming, they sat on the water's edge, and watched it steadily recede. "I'd better move the boat," said Porter. "She's almost aground."

Sarah watched as the boy walked through in the shallow water. *He looks different, not just taller, but more muscular. I suppose I look different, too.* Sarah patted her hair, now wet and straight. *It didn't do much good to sleep on bobby pins last night*, she decided. Hair styles, make up, and cute outfits seemed lost on this boy. In order to keep up with Porter, a girl needed jeans, sneakers and a head start. Sarah stared at the ripples of water around her legs. *I'll be a tom boy today,* she vowed. *Tonight will be different when he sees my new white dress. Maybe I can get Granny Jewel to put my hair up in a style like Betty Grable.*

Her thoughts were interrupted by a call from Porter. "Sarah, I'm starving! Did you bring me over here to watch me slowly die of hunger?"

Sarah grinned and waved. "I'm coming. Try not to faint until I can get the food ready."

Together they walked from the beach to an area of small scrub oak trees. "There's not much shade here, but it's better than nothing," said Sarah.

"I don't care if there's shade or not. I'm hungry!"

"You don't need to be in the sun much longer," she cautioned. "Your skin's not tough. If you get a bad sun burn, you'll be in so much pain, you won't be able to sleep. You could even run a fever."

"I don't plan to be sick this week. I want to spend every minute I can with you."

Sarah, unwrapping deviled eggs and ham sandwiches, gave the boy a side long glance. "I enjoy being with you, too." The thought of Porter leaving at the end of the week was too painful to imagine.

The picnic basket empty, and scraps thrown to hungry gulls, the couple relaxed in the sun dappled shade. A distant thud of boat engines and muffled sounds from across the creek, combined to make Sarah and Porter feel alone.

Sarah turned to her friend. "Porter, what are your dreams for the future?" She gazed steadily, hoping he would not tease.

The young man snapped the stem of a nearby sea oat and chewed the end. "For the first two years I'll be taking regular college courses. My junior and senior years, if I don't flunk out, I'll major in aeronautical engineering. When I graduate, I want to join the Marine Corps and become a fighter pilot."

"That sounds very exciting," commented Sarah, drawing in the hard packed sand.

"How about you, Sarah? What do you want to be when you grow up?" He smiled leaned over and pulled a lock of her hair.

"I don't know, Porter. I've been thinking of a lot of things, but nothing seems to really interest me. I may want to go to secretarial school, be a teacher, or study chemistry at State College. I could work in my father's chemical plant in Raleigh."

"Aren't you afraid you might blow something up?" Sarah glanced sideways, ready with a quick retort.

"The army awards my father contracts to invent ways to blow things up."

"I'll bet you'll meet a nice fellow, fall in love and get married."

Sarah buried her toes in the sand. "I do want to get married some day, but, I want to do something exciting first."

Porter reached for her hand, brushing off fine, white sand. "Some day I may come riding up on a white horse and ask for your hand in marriage, even if I have to brush sand off of it."

"Porter, I declare, my first real marriage proposal, and you have to make it a big joke!" Sarah grabbed the picnic basket. "Let's look in tidal pools on the mud flats. Soon the tide will start in, and they'll be covered."

They walked along the edge of the water, their feet sinking in cool, soft mud. Porter, carrying the basket, reached for Sarah's hand.

"I remember these little tidal pools," said Porter, looking across the wide expanse of shore.

"My grandfather says it's from flounder that lie here at night during high tide." Sarah knelt over one pool. "Oh, look, Porter. There are minnows and baby blue crabs in this one."

Porter looked sad. "I feel sorry for them. They're trapped and have no way out."

"No, silly," Sarah explained. "The incoming tide will free them." Sarah stood, looking worried. "We need to go. You're getting too much sun." Without another word, she turned and walked toward the boat. "Come on, Porter. A bad sunburn could be serious."

"Yes, dear, whatever you say." Once more he pulled a lock of her hair. "It sounds like we're married already."

A cool shower was refreshing after the heat and sticky salt water. Sarah sat on the upstairs front porch letting her hair dry. When she stepped inside, she stopped at her grandmother's bedroom. "Granny Jewel, would you put my hair up this evening? When I try, some strands keep teasing out. You seem to have some magic power when it comes to hair."

Jewel Mitchell laughed. "I'd be delighted, honey. Why don't you sit at my vanity and we'll get started." Once again Sarah drank in the delicate, lavender fragrance that always seemed to follow her grandmother. Her sure, deft movements transformed the thick, dark hair from straight and limp, to stylish and dramatic. "Remember the combs that belonged to your great-grandmother?" From a small drawer in the vanity, she produced ivory combs Sarah had worn before on special occasions.

"I do remember them, Granny Jewel. They belonged to great-grandmother Frances." Sarah leaned forward, speaking in a whisper. "With my hair up, my eyes look bigger."

"Yes, and you look ten years older," observed the grandmother sadly. "Sarah," she said wistfully, "I feel I looked away for a moment, and you grew up. Where is my little girl in pig tails?"

Sarah turned and grabbed her grandmother around the waist. "I'm here, Granny Jewel! I'll always be here, and I'll always be your little granddaughter, no matter how old I get."

Sarah slipped the crisp white dress over her head, careful not to disturb her hair. The full skirt accentuated her small waist, the bodice flattering her soft, rounded bust. Slipping on her white sandals, Sarah twirled before the mirror. *He won't forget tonight, even when he goes home*, she thought. Sarah smiled at her reflection. *I won't forget, either.*

"Hubba, hubba," exclaimed Papa Tom catching sight of his granddaughter. He sat up, taking his attention from the radio program. "I don't know where you're going tonight, but I'm going, too!"

"Oh, Papa, Porter and I are going to the picture show. There is a double feature tonight, so I'll be a little bit late."

"Peggy," called the grandfather, "are you going to entrust our beautiful girl to some young fellow for the whole evening? Why can't they stay here with the family?"

"For the same reason you and I loved to steal away and be by ourselves fifty years ago," said Granny Jewel. A knock on the front door interrupted their conversation.

"I'll get it!" said Sarah, springing from the chair. Rushing to the front door, Sarah was dismayed to see it was not Porter. "*Bruce!*" she exclaimed. Confused, she blurted, "What are you doing here?"

"Aren't you going to invite me in?" the boy asked, also confused.

"Uh, it's much cooler out here." Quickly, she stepped outside and walked to the edge of the porch. Bruce followed, taking her hand. She slipped it away and quickly touched her hair.

Bruce took a step closer. "You look very beautiful tonight, Sarah. Is that a new dress?"

"Yes, it's new," she replied, keeping a watchful eye in the direction of the Inlet Inn.

"Did you wear it especially for our date tonight?"

Sarah turned, eyes wide. "*Date?*" she asked, incredulously.

"Yes, Sarah," he replied impatiently. "You know we always date on Friday night. It's our special time." He took a step backward. "Did you *forget?*"

"I guess I did, Bruce. I forgot it was Friday." Sarah, feeling ashamed, studied her sandals.

"Then why are you all dressed up?"

"Well, I have to go to the movies tonight with my company."

"You mean you **want** to go to the movies with your company."

Sarah's back straightened, "He's my friend. We're known each other for years, and, what if I do want to go to the movies with him!" Hands on hips, head tilted, she narrowed her eyes and drew her lips in a thin line "There's nothing wrong with that!"

"Yes." said Bruce, raising his voice, "There is something wrong with that! You're **my** girl, not his. Everybody in town has seen you with that red-haired boy, and you act like he's a lot more than a friend."

Sarah had no quick reply. When the silence was too much, she whispered, "I'm sorry, Bruce, but this is the way it is. Next week he'll be gone, and . . .

"And so will I, Sarah. Don't think for a minute I'm going to sit around and wait for **him** to leave so you'll be my girl again." Bruce stepped off the porch and cut across the front lawn. "Goodbye, Sarah," he said, choking on her name.

Sarah turned, yanked open the screen door and hurried to her room.

In the living room, the grandparents' eyes met. Papa Tom slowly shook his head. "Bruce may be the first, but he surely won't be the last who's heart she'll break."

Clara appeared in the doorway. "What ails that girl now? She flew past me with never a word like, 'goodnight, Clara, or I love you, Clara, or kiss my foot, Clara.'"

"It's problems of the heart. You'll have to overlook her behavior."

Clara's eyes narrowed. "Has one of those sorry boys hurt my baby's feelings?"

"No, Clara. It's the other way around," offered Papa Tom. "She just gave Bruce his walking papers." He shook his head. "I feel sorry for the poor lad."

"A broken heart never killed anybody. He'll survive," Clara said without sympathy. "I remember when my mama was working for your mama, Jewel Mitchell. There were young fellows hanging around the house, getting their hearts broken every day. Why you picked the skinniest, sorriest looking one of the bunch, has always been a mystery to me." She turned her head slowly, eyes resting on Papa Tom.

"Now, Clara, you know the lovely Jewel Harris had no defenses against my charm and rugged good looks."

"I've had all this I can stand for one day. I'm going home." Clara turned and moved down the hall. A moment later, they heard the sound of someone knocking. *R-a-tat-tat, rat-a-tat-tat.* It was a sound that had become familiar to all.

"Mama," whispered Peggy, "I'll tell Sarah her date is here, if you'll go to the door." Peggy hurried to her daughter's room. *I hope she's not too upset*, thought Peggy. *If her eyes and nose are red from crying, he'll know something's wrong.* The mother tapped lightly on her daughter's door.

"Come in," was Sarah's muffled reply.

"Honey, are you all right?"

"Sure, Mama," Sarah answered brightly. "Is Porter here?"

"Yes, he just arrived." Sarah checked her lipstick once more and brushed past her mother, leaving a wave of delicate cologne.

"You're not upset, are you," Peggy called.

"Upset? Why would I be upset?" Sarah glanced over her shoulder, flashing her mother a look of pure happiness.

Chapter 15

Sarah awoke with a sense of dread. For a moment she could not remember why. She stared at the ceiling as the awful truth dawned. This was Porter's last day. Tomorrow he and his parents would be returning to Ohio. Tears welled, coursing along the side of her face, dampening the snow white bed linens. Even Mr. Peavy's insistent voice seemed mournful and off key.

I don't think I can stand to see him leave. I'll never laugh or be happy again. She turned on her side and curled into a tiny knot. The idea of returning to Raleigh and resuming a life of school, sports, cheerleading and friends seemed remote and unreal.

It had been a wonderful week. The day before, they packed a picnic lunch and took Joshua and Amy to Atlantic Beach to play in the surf. On Sunday, they attended St. Paul's Episcopal Church. Porter had been given a hero's welcome. Teens clustered around him, with Nancy giving him a welcome hug that lasted much too long. The adults remembered the lad who had been an acolyte one summer during the war. They spent hours in Capt. Jake's dock house listening to the old gentleman spin tales of growing up on the waterfront.

The aroma of fried bacon drifted under her bedroom door. Clara could be heard in the next room, preparing breakfast. As Sarah was deciding which cute outfit to wear, a sharp wrap came on the door. "Your breakfast is getting cold, sleeping beauty," announced Clara. "If you're going to court day and night, you gotta keep your strength up."

"Clara, you know I don't date day and night. Mama is strict about my eleven o'clock curfew," said Sarah, helping put the meal on the table.

"Come along now, Amy," said her mother. Amy, refusing help, carefully descended each step. At three and one half, the child was already showing her independence. By the time Amy was securely fastened in her chair, the rest of the family had arrived. "What are you and Porter going to do today, honey?" asked the mother, scooping pulp from half a grapefruit.

"We're going to explore the dungeons at Fort Macon."

"Be careful, Sarah. Tide rises in the moat, and there is no light in the dungeons.

"I want to go! I want to go!" exclaimed Joshua, fork poised in mid air. "I want to look for pirate bones."

"It's true the fort was built to keep pirates from attacking Beaufort, but I don't think their remains are still there," said Papa Tom.

"I want to go anyway. Mackie wants to go, too."

"Me too! Me, too!" echoed Amy between spoonfuls of cream of wheat. Her hand clutched a strip of bacon, squeezed almost in half. Sarah looked away. It was too painful to watch a three year old feed herself. Sarah wondered briefly what life would be like if she were an only child.

"Be home in plenty of time to get cleaned up for dinner. Porter and his parents are our guests tonight," reminded Granny Jewel.

After exploring what had been barracks, offices and other rooms, the couple found themselves at the top of the fort, overlooking Beaufort Inlet. Weary from so much walking, Sarah perched on top of a cannon which had once fired on pirate ships. "This fort has protected the people of Beaufort and Morehead City during several wars. After pirates, it protected us from the British, then the Yankees during the Civil War, and finally, the Germans in two world wars."

"You would make a terrific tour guide, Sarah," said Porter, stretching full length on the grass in the shade cast by the huge cannon.

Sarah shaded her eyes with one hand, and looked across the inlet. On the far side was the tip of Shackleford Banks, part of the outer banks of North Carolina. In the distance, on a clear day, Cape Lookout lighthouse was visible. Sarah couldn't see it today, a mist of tears obstructed her view. "Today is passing too quickly," she said softly, to the tall, handsome fellow smiling up at her. Suddenly, his smile faded. He was beside her in an instant.

"Sarah," he said, turning her face with one hand. "Someday I'll be back. I promise. It's important that I go to college, and you finish high school. We're too young to make a serious commitment."

Sarah sighed. "I know all that, but it doesn't help."

In an effort to cheer her, he made a silly face. "Now, don't you go and fall for somebody else while my back is turned."

"Porter Mason, you'll be flirting with college girls while I'm sitting in a boring algebra class. I'll be the farthest thing from your mind."

"That's not true, Sarah. I'll think about you every day."

Sarah laughed and gave him a playful shove. "Oh, sure."

"I have something to prove how I feel," he said seriously. "but I can't give it to you here."

"Why not?" asked the girl, mystified.

"You'll understand when we get there."

Neither spoke during the ride home, each deep in thought. When Porter stopped in front of St. Paul's Episcopal Church, Sarah's eyes widened. "Oh, Porter, I know what you're thinking!"

The couple, holding hands, hurried to the cemetery behind the old church. They stopped beneath a towering oak, its limbs spreading across several cemetery plots. "Thank goodness no one has cut our tree down," said Porter, sounding relieved.

"Thank goodness a hurricane hasn't uprooted it," added Sarah.

"Follow me," volunteered Porter, "so you won't fall." Soon they were sitting on the same wide limbs where they sat years before. Sarah ran her hand across the rough, uncomfortable bark of the tree. It hadn't improved with time.

"It's just as I remembered it," said Porter, dreamily. "The sounds below seem so distant."

"No one knows we're here," she added.

Porter's expression saddened. "And tomorrow, we won't be."

Sarah felt as if a great weight was on her chest, keeping her from taking a deep breath. Fearing she might cry, the girl only nodded.

Porter reached in his pocket and produced a heart-shaped box. "I went to Bell's Jewelry store and found something for you, Sarah. Even though we'll be a thousand miles apart, I hope when you wear it, you'll think of me."

Porter offered the gift in his outstretched hand. Dappled sunlight shone on the rose-colored box, making it glow. Sarah was surprised at the soft, smooth feel of the velvet cover. She looked up, eyes meeting his. "I don't have a going away present for you, Porter. I'm sorry."

"This is not exactly a going away gift. It's something that will make me feel close to you if I think you're wearing it."

Sarah slowly opened the hinged box. Inside, gleaming in the partial sunlight, was a ring made of tiny gold hearts. While she was staring, Porter gently took it from the box and placed it on her ring finger. Sarah held up her hand, staring at the shining band encircling her finger. "It's beautiful, Porter. I promise I'll wear it every day."

"I don't know when we'll be together again. I'll be in school and working part time. Maybe I can save a little money and come back for a few days next summer."

The thoughts of not seeing this wonderful boy for a whole year grieved Sarah. "Will you write to me?" she asked.

Porter grinned, the dappled sunlight playing across freckles across his nose. "I'll try, Sarah, but you know I'm not good at writing letters."

Sarah laughed. "Yeah, I remember a lot of my letters went unanswered.

Porter took her hand and slid onto the branch beside Sarah. "You'll always be my favorite girl," he whispered, kissing her tenderly. They sat together for a time, neither wanting to leave.

Later, Sarah looked at her watch. "Wow, I didn't realize it was getting late. I need to go home and help Mama and Granny Jewel. If I'm not there, Amy is going to help."

Dinner preparations were underway when Sarah got home. A white damask cloth covered the table, silver candelabra on either side of a bouquet of late summer flowers. Sterling silver flatware was at each place setting, gleaming in the late afternoon shafts of sunlight coming in the tall windows. Sarah stood for a moment admiring the scene. *My granny really knows how to entertain*, she thought. *Someday I must get her to teach me.* Voices in the kitchen drew her attention.

"Sarah, is that you?" asked Granny Jewel. "Amy is up from her nap, and your mama is upstairs with her. Wash your hands and come stir the gravy. Roast beef is better with gravy, so don't let it lump."

"Why aren't we having seafood? They probably can't get fresh ocean fish in Ohio."

"Barbara told your mama they've had seafood every night, and roast beef would be a pleasant change."

When the gravy was safely made, with only a few lumps, Sarah took a quick shower, and put on Nancy's borrowed dress. Nancy would be wearing her white dress on her date with Henry. After several attempts at putting up her hair, she decided to sweep it back on each side with her grandmother's ivory combs. Carefully she applied rouge, lipstick and powder. Her only jewelry was earrings and her gold ring.

Conversation at the table was lively among the older people. While Papa Tom and Porter's father talked business, the ladies discussed fall fashions. Porter and Sarah sat across from each other, speaking with their eyes. Evening shadows turned to night. An electric fan sitting in one corner was turned on when the breeze dropped. By nine o'clock, the Masons said their goodbyes and walked back to the Inlet Inn. Porter and Sarah walked to the far end of the porch.

"I have to go now, Sarah," Porter whispered. "We want to get on the road early, and I don't want to fall asleep at the wheel."

"I don't want you to leave."

"I'll be back someday," he whispered, gathering her in his arms. He kissed her upturned lips, then gently pushed her away, and hurried from the porch. Pausing for a moment he turned and called, "Don't forget me, Sarah." The street light on the corner showed the back of his tall figure. He moved through the circle of light and was swallowed by the darkness.

For several minutes, Sarah remained motionless. She stared at the place where she had last seen the boy who touched her heart as no other had.

The spell was broken when Peggy opened the screen door. "Sarah, we can't leave this mess for Clara. You're needed in the kitchen."

Numbly, Sarah moved across the porch, bumping into a chair. "He's gone, Mama. Porter's gone."

"I know, honey," said the mother, putting a protective arm around her daughter's drooping shoulders. "I know it hurts. Matters of the heart always hurt. I'd rather have a tummy ache than a heart ache any time."

Sarah started to get up the following morning, gave up, turned over and faced the wall. There was no reason to get up, she decided. Her life was over. She listened for sounds from the rest of the house, knowing it was late by the sunlight streaming in the tiny window. Slowly, she dragged herself out of bed. She stood uncertainly, turned and sat heavily on the edge of the bed. Elbows on knees, chin propped on fists, she closed her eyes and groaned. *There is no reason to get up today.* She fell back and stared, unseeing, at the ceiling. A light tap on the door reminded her she was still among the living.

"Come in," she said in a dull voice. The door opened cautiously. She could see only one eye peeping through the crack. It was her brother.

"What do you want," she asked not too unkindly.

The door opened wider. "You didn't come to breakfast, Sarah. Mama said to let you sleep as long as you wanted to." Joshua eased onto the edge of the bed beside his sister. "You never looked so strange, even when you had flu last winter. Do you have a temperature?" He put his hand on his sister's forehead, as he had seen his mother do countless times. "No," he said, shaking his head slowly. "You don't have a fever."

"Thank you, Dr. Bowers, for your diagnosis." Sarah smiled weakly and put her arm around Joshua, drawing him closer. "What are you going to do today? Maybe we could pal around together."

A worried expression crossed his face. "I'm going to Piver's Island and play with Katie. Pretty soon her mother is going to have a baby."

He sighed deeply. "You know what that means, no more play—just work, work, work."

"Yeah, brother, we know all about that." They sat in companionable silence, each remembering how their lives changed when Amy was born.

"Katie stomps around her house, yells whenever she feels like it, and lets the door slam when she goes out."

"All that will soon stop," declared Sarah.

"You bet." Joshua stood suddenly. "Katie's mother is picking me up after she runs errands in town. She'll be here soon, so, I'm going to sit on the porch and wait." He rested his hand on the door knob and turned. "I hope you'll feel better."

"Thanks, brother."

A tall glass of orange juice, a boiled egg and buttered toast made Sarah feel well enough to get dressed. *I'll call Nancy and see if we can do something. Maybe we can window shop, or go to the movies.*

Mrs. Cora answered. "Nancy's not here, honey. A group of teenagers from the church have gone to Camp Leach for a few days. This year they are counselors for the younger children."

Mrs. Cora's words made Sarah feel even more lonely. "Mama!" she called at the foot of the steps. Her mother's face appeared over the banister. "Would you like me to take Amy for a ride in the stroller?" Sarah could hear relief in her mother's voice. "That would be grand. I'm trying to sort the clothes we're not wearing and get them ready to pack." A few days earlier, these words would have caused a feeling of sadness. Now, it would be a welcome change to get back to Raleigh. *At least I won't be reminded of Porter everywhere I look.*

Amy, excited about an outing, eagerly climbed into the stroller. "Now, baby sister, we're going to head for Front Street and the cool ocean breeze. We can look at boats on the waterfront."

"Sing, Sarah, sing," chanted Amy, smiling at her big sister.

"I will if you promise not to stand up in the stroller." Sadly, Sarah knew she wouldn't fit in it another summer.

"Mama, Mama, have you heard," Sarah sang.

"Daddy's gonna' buy me a mockingbird," answered Amy. They strolled the length of Front Street, ending at Capt. Jake's dock. "We can visit Capt. Jake for a few minutes, if you promise to hold my hand."

"I promise," said Amy, struggling to free herself.

"Well, would you look a-here!" greeted Capt. Jake as they walked the length of the dock. He extended a rough, sun burned hand. "What's your name, little lady?" he asked, giving them one of his rare smiles. His face, weathered by the sun, wind and a generous amount of time, resembled the leather of her mother's winter hand bag.

"Come in the dock house and sit for a spell," he offered. They walked through the tiny room perched on the end of the wide dock. A breeze rushed through, cooling the room. When they were seated on wooden deck chairs, Capt. Jake tipped back his hat and took a battered pipe from his shirt pocket. From another, he produced a pouch of tobacco. Sarah knew from summers past, conversation ceased, and all waited while the captain packed and lit his weathered pipe. Then, conversation could continue. Amy, fascinated with the operation, left Sarah's side, and sat beside the old man. Not observing the respectful silence, she said, "Santa Claus has a pipe like that." Looking closely at Capt. Jake's white whiskers, she asked, "Are you Santa Claus?"

Capt. Jake threw back his head and laughed. "I've been mistaken for a lot of things, but never Santa Claus."

"It must be getting close to time for you all to go back to Raleigh," said Capt. Jake through puffs.

"Yes, sir, we only have a few days left." From the corner of her eye she saw a familiar white sail in the channel. "Oh, there's Bruce!"

She hurried out to the end of the dock. "Hi, Bruce," she called, waving. *Maybe I'll get to go sailing again before we have to go home*, she thought.

The boy, hearing his name, sat up and turned. When he did, Sarah saw another head in the boat. Sarah recognized Paula Jones, one of the girls in her Sunday school class. Bruce barely waved and turned his attention once more to the cute girl snuggled beside him. Before Sarah stepped back in the boathouse, she saw him put an arm around the girl, just as he had done when they went sailing. The sight made Sarah feel hollow inside. As they sailed on down the channel, Paula looked adoringly at Bruce, and whispered in his ear. Both laughed at the shared secret.

Sarah stepped back inside the boat house, slumped in the chair, feeling she didn't have a friend in the world. Capt. Jake's pipe was now in high gear. Amy sat motionless watching the smoke coming from the marvelous instrument.

Capt. Jake watched Sarah as he puffed. Squinting one eye, he said, "That Bruce is a mighty fine lad and a good sailor."

"I know."

"It's a pity how you cast him aside when that red-headed boy showed up. 'Dropped him like a hot potato,' some folks said."

"It didn't take long for him to find someone to mend his broken heart," answered Sarah. She watched a stream of silver smoke, borne on the south wind, float through the front door.

"Why, no. Most any girl in this town, or the next, would give her eye teeth to sail with Bruce aboard the **Willa**."

Sarah gave him a curious look. "How did you know, Captain Jake?"

"It don't take long for word to get around in a little town like Beaufort."

Sarah stared glumly at the toe of her sneaker. "I didn't think there'd be any harm in being with Porter while he was here on vacation."

Capt. Jake puffed mightily, fearful the fire in his pipe would die. "I got a feeling someday, when the two of you come of age, you and that red haired boy will get hitched. There's been something special between you two ever since you were in pigtails."

A certain peace came over Sarah, a feeling of contentment. 'When we come of age,' Capt. Jake said. Not now. Not any time soon. Now is the time for parties, new clothes, football games and dates, lots of dates with different boys.

Sarah took Amy's hand. She looked down at the old gentleman sitting contentedly on the wooden bench. "I learned one thing this summer, Capt. Jake. If I have a date, with one boy, I'll never break it to be with someone else, not if it's the president's son!"

Capt. Jake stared at a small detail across the channel, his eyes tiny slits. "You've learned an important lesson. Life will teach you plenty more before you're my age."

That night, Sarah's tears dried earlier than the night before. The next morning she joined the family at breakfast. While conversation flowed around her, Sarah nibbled at her food, sighing between each bite.

"Sarah, honey, what's wrong?" asked her grandfather. "Where's my girl's million dollar smile?"

"It's gone. She sent it home with that aggrivatin' boy," interrupted Clara, armed with a pot of hot coffee. "Now she's all droopy-fied."

"I can't help how I feel!"

Close to tears, Sarah left the table, hurried through the kitchen and out the back door. *Nobody in this house understands. My mother and grandparents are too old to remember what it's like to be in love, and my brother and sister are too young. I wish I was in Raleigh so I could call Lindsay. She would understand.*

Sarah reached up, her hand closing over the tiny heart-shaped rhinestone necklace. "Bruce, Bruce," she murmured. "I'm so sorry I hurt you. I hope someday you'll be able to forgive me."

Sarah heard the screen door close. Looking up she saw her grandmother walking toward her.

"The swing looks mighty lonesome this morning. Why don't we sit down and visit for a few minutes."

Unable to think of an excuse, Sarah nodded. She sat down beside her grandmother, sighed deeply, and looked up at the leafy boughs overhead. *Oh, brother. Now I'll have to listen to some tale of heartache my granny overcame a million years ago.* Immediately she felt disloyal for having such a thought about the woman she most wanted to be like.

"Sometimes I get so bored." began Granny Jewel. "When that happens, I get my mind off myself by helping someone else. For instance, this morning the Episcopal Church Women are having a white elephant sale at the church. We're raising money for a young man who wants to attend seminary, but hasn't the money for tuition. The whole day will be filled with sorting and selling items people have donated. We're expecting quite a crowd of people because our sales have become famous among the townspeople. The only problem is, we're a little short handed, because a lot of people are on vacation."

Jewel Mitchell cast a side-long glance at her granddaughter. "Your mama and Mary Stewart wanted to help, but they have small children. To tell the truth, it would do them both a world of good to get away for a few hours. If *only* they had someone to watch the girls."

Sarah turned to her grandmother. "I could do that, Granny Jewel. I could watch the girls. I'll take them to the shore and let them play in the sand. We'll take a picnic lunch. When we get home, I'll give them a bath and read stories."

Sarah began to brighten, enthusiasm in her voice. "I'll go tell mama to call Mary so they can make plans." Sarah smiled at her grandmother. "I know you're helping fill in the gap, Granny Jewel, and I appreciate it. Sometimes you have to fill the gap yourself."

The grandmother's eyes misted. "Sarah Bowers, you are a blessing from God none of us earned. You are a gift."

"He also gave me the best family a person could ever have."

Chapter 16

"Come along, girls," said Sarah, a slight edge in her voice. Hmmm, three year olds have no sense of time, she decided. Her arms were loaded with beach towels, sun tan lotion, shirts, hats, sun glasses and a picnic basket with food enough for a truck driver.

Perspiration trickled down Sarah's back and stood on her hands and arms, causing them to be slippery. *If I drop this load, I'll never get it all picked up. It will just have to stay here, a great mound in the middle of the sidewalk.* She started to bark a command at the two, but the sharp words died as she watched the pair move slowly along. Tiny toes, in sandals now too small, resembled perfect rows of corn kernels. Both wore sailor caps, brims turned down, and brightly colored bathing suits. Dimpled elbows and knees begged a kiss. *Next time I'll use the wagon*, Sarah decided, then realized there may not be a next time this summer.

When they were in sight of sparkling blue water, Laney spotted a shiny black bug scurrying across the sidewalk. She let out a piercing scream. "A bug! A bug, Sarah! Save me!

Sarah knelt beside the terrified child. In her most soothing tone, she said, "Laney, honey, that little bug isn't going to hurt you. Uh . . . he's hurrying home because he misses his mama."

"Me, too! Me too!" chanted Amy. "I want my mama," she wailed, close to tears.

Laney, watching Amy, tuned up and began to cry. "I want my mama," she wailed, heartbroken.

"Girls, *please* don't cry. Our mamas will be home soon." Under her breath she added, "I hope." These words quieted the girls. "The little fishes in the creek are waiting to meet you. They'll be disappointed if we go back home." The thoughts of a creek full of fish waiting just for them stilled the girls' longing.

Several mothers were already sitting on the shore, their children laughing and splashing in the shallow water. The beach looked as if a moving van had backed down to the shore and unloaded.

Sarah dropped her burden on the white sand, and feeling returned to her arms. Carefully, she spread towels on the hot sand, and scrambled in the picnic basket for a bottle of sun tan lotion. The girls, skin glistening, were happily playing with their brightly colored metal buckets and shovels. Sarah took this opportunity to catch her breath and try to recover from the grueling journey of one block.

"Don't go out too deep," the big sister cautioned. *I sound like mama,* she realized, smiling. Amy, not fearing the water, had to be watched every second. Laney seemed content to dig in the sand. Blue sky, sea green water lapping on the shore and the distant cry of shore birds all conspired to give Sarah a sense of peace and contentment. *I'll take this scene with me when we leave,* she determined. *On bitter cold days, when concrete, tall buildings and asphalt are all the eye can see, I'll return to this moment in my mind.* Leaving Beaufort and her grandparents was the hardest thing she did each year. *Someday, someday,* she vowed, *I'll come back and stay for good. When the summer people leave, I'll smile and wave goodbye.*

Sarah watched as Amy filled her bucket with water. She waded up on the shore and, before Sarah could move, poured the contents on

Laney's head. The child, too surprised to move, favored all with an ear piercing scream.

"No, no, Amy," yelled Sarah, too late. She hurried across the sand to the heartbroken child. Water dripped from Laney's hat, chin and nose. Her screams turned to wailing sobs.

"Amy! Look what you've done! You've made Laney very unhappy." *Also, a beach full of peace-loving people*, thought Sarah.

Amy, lower lip out, defended her actions. "I watered Laney so she would grow."

"Where did you get such an idea?" asked the big sister.

"Daddy says you have to water things if you want them to grow."

"Laney is *not* a plant!"

"Yes, she is!" insisted Amy, stamping her foot.

"Where did you get *that* idea?"

Amy looked accusingly at her little friend, who managed to climb in Sarah's lap.

"Your answer better be good."

"Miss Mary calls her, 'precious flower.'"

"I am my mama's precious flower. She says so every day."

Amy unused to seeing another child in her big sister's lap, became jealous.

"I want Laney to go home." Again, Amy's lower lip protruded.

Sarah could see their outing rapidly coming unglued. She knew that desperate times call for desperate measures. "Oh, I want to grow, too! HURRY, Amy, water your big sister. The hot sun is making me wilt!"

Slowly, a smile came on the little sister's face. She hurried to the water's edge, scooped a bucket full of water, and poured it on her sister's head. Laney scrambled to get out of the way, not anxious to be watered again. Both stood for a moment, unsure of Sarah's reaction.

Hair dripping, the big sister sputtered, wiped salt water from her face and arms and grinned. "Oh, my! I feel taller already!" she squealed. "Thank you, Amy."

Laney, catching the spirit of the moment declared, "I'm going to grow Amy!" Quickly, she dumped sand from her bucket, filled it, and watered Amy from head to toe. The shock of cool water on hot skin made Amy catch her breath. When she could speak, she said determinedly, "I'm going to water Laney **real** good." When she stooped to fill her bucket, Laney did the same.

What have I started? wondered Sarah. *Could this be World War III?* This all-out declaration of war could only end in tears. "I'm shrinking! I'm shrinking," Sarah called pitifully. I need more water!" The girls, declaring a silent truce, turned their combined efforts on Sarah, gleefully soaking her. Salt water dripped off her hair, eyes burning from the salt. Hardly able to catch her breath, Sarah held her arms up, surrendering. *So what*, she thought, *this day can't last forever,*

Before Sarah could dry her face, Laney announced, "I'm hungry. Feed me, please."

"Me, too! Me, too," echoed Amy.

Sarah was once more in charge. "Girls, sit on this nice, dry towel, and I'll unwrap the peanut butter and jelly sandwiches." Both walked across the clean towel with sandy feet. Amy looked at her big sister. "I can't sit here, it's sandy."

"Sit!" ordered the big sister, a sticky sandwich in each hand. Jelly, attempting to escape, gave the bread a purple hue.

"There's sand on my fingers," wailed Laney, trying to rub it off with the already gritty towel. Sarah balanced both sandwiches in one hand, and retrieved a stack of napkins. "Wipe your hands, and you'll be fine," she said soothingly. She smiled serenely at the young children while perspiration trickled from every crevice of her body.

While the girls were occupied with their sandwiches, Sarah grabbed another from the basket, whipped off the wax paper, and stuffed it in her mouth. Cheeks puffed, she swallowed the sandwich in three gulps. *I have to eat fast before the next disaster*, she thought.

"I'm so thirsty," whined Amy.

"My sandwich is crunchy," complained Laney, holding it in a vice-like grip, jelly escaping between chubby fingers.

"Sh-sh-sh," hissed Sarah. "If the other children know you have crunchy jelly, they'll cry because theirs is plain. "Laney, happy to be part of a conspiracy, ate the rest of her sandwich in silence.

"Clara made our lemonade, girls, so, I know it's just right." Sarah handed each a cup. While the girls drank, Sarah, in her advanced state of dehydration, tipped the thermos and drank deeply. Animal crackers completed the picnic, each girl identifying an animal before biting its head off.

The long walk home proved to be more strenuous than the morning. All were sandy and sticky from salt water. The sun beat mercilessly on their heads and shoulders. When Sarah felt they could not take another step, a truck pulled alongside. "Anybody need a lift?" Sarah looked up into her uncle's smiling face.

"Uncle Herb! Oh, yes, we need a lift badly."

Herb Mitchell opened the door on the panel truck, scooped a girl in each arm, and put them in the back. Next, he took the bundle of towels, toys and picnic basket from Sarah's aching arms. "Your white shirt is wet and sandy now, Uncle Herb."

"Hey, it's worth it to get to hold such adorable kids, and to help a weary aunt." He grinned at Sarah as she climbed in beside the girls.

"I thought Amy was a handful, but *two* is almost more than a person can handle."

"Folks do what they have to do," replied Uncle Herb. Sarah nodded wearily, neither realizing how true these words would someday be.

"Run inside and fill the tub. I'll bring the girls," commanded the uncle, taking charge of the operation. "I'll put your wet towels and other stuff on the back porch because everything is sandy."

Sarah gladly followed her uncle's orders. Soon warm water filled the bottom of the tub. Herb Mitchell's footsteps were heard on the stairs. He appeared in the doorway, a weary child in each arm. Sarah peeled off their wet, sandy suits and lowered them in the warm water.

"Uncle Herb, you'll never know how thankful I was to see you today."

"Always ready to help a damsel in distress, especially if she happens to be my gorgeous niece." He turned to leave. "I have to hurry. Miss Nettie won't want her ice cream to turn to soup."

Sarah smiled. "Miss Nettie would never complain."

"No, she would toss her head and insist she's loves eating warm ice cream because it has such a wondrous texture."

Sarah hurried the girls through their bath, wrapped each in a thick, white towel and took them into the bedroom. "Nap time, nap time," she announced triumphantly. Dressed in clean, dry clothes, the girls stretched out on the bed. "Does anyone need something to drink, or potty, or *anything* that might interfere with nap time?" They answered Sarah with solemn stares, eye lids heavy. Sarah eased toward the door. "Now, take a nice long nap. When you wake up, your mamas will be here."

Amy sat up, ramrod straight. "You have to read a story, or we can't get to sleep." Sarah glanced toward the book shelf, knowing she had lost another round.

"Which book?" She asked wearily.

"Raggedy Ann in the Deep, Deep Woods," Amy replied, grinning.

Sarah found the worn, loved copy. Carrying it to the bed, she nestled between the girls. They smelled of fragrant shampoo and Camay soap. Sarah kissed each on the top of their head. Little children, she observed, were much easier to love when they smelled good.

"Raggedy Ann and Raggedy Andy were sitting under a tree in the deep, deep woods, filled with fairies 'n' everything, drinking a glass of soda water through two straws."

After the first page, Sarah realized her eyelids were made of lead. Reading a whole sentence without yawning was impossible. The heavy, even breathing of the girls made her more relaxed. Gently she lowered the book and closed her eyes.

Later, when the mothers returned, they found three girls sleeping peacefully in the cool, dark room.

After supper, dishes done, Sarah and her mother stepped out on the front porch to enjoy the cool evening breeze. "How was your day, honey?" the mother asked.

"It was fun, Mama, but I wouldn't want to do it *every* day. I don't know how you have the strength." She gave her mother an admiring look.

"Someday, when you have babes of your own, it will be the most natural thing on earth." After a few minutes of silence, Peggy gave her daughter a side long glance. "I know you miss Porter, but each day will get a little easier."

"You're right, Mama." Sarah wearily tucked a strand of hair behind her ear. "Today was much easier. I didn't have time to give him a single thought."

The next morning, Sarah decided to return library books. The old train depot, with its interesting architecture, plus the distinct smell of books always made her want to linger after books had been checked out. Today would be different. She would not be checking out books.

It would be months before she would be back. Raleigh had many libraries, some several stories high, and five times bigger. Still, Sarah preferred this small, quaint building.

As she neared her grandparents' home, she noticed a strange car parked in front. *It must be one of my granny's friends I haven't met.* Ladies were forever calling on or telephoning her beautiful, vivacious grandmother. *It seems impossible that someday my grandparents will be old and feeble, like other people's grandparents. However I can't think about that—it's too painful.*

Sarah heard her grandmother's voice as she opened the screen door. "Sarah," she called, "Come here, honey. You have company."

"Me," she muttered, "who would come visit me?"

In the living room, enjoying cookies and ice cold lemonade, were Janie and Mike Lawrence. As she stepped in, Mike hurriedly rose to his feet. From the corner of her eye, she saw another quickly rise. It was their son, Samuel. She felt a rush of pleasure at seeing the tall, good looking young man. Today his blonde curly hair was not hidden by a hat, as it had when they met. He smiled, and shook her hand, deep brown eyes never leaving her face.

"Sarah, you look as if you need something cold to drink," observed her grandmother.

"Yes, Ma'am. It's really hot today."

Sarah sipped a frosted glass of the cold, sweet liquid. While Peggy and the Lawrence's entertained Granny Jewel with the circumstance of how they met, Sarah could feel Samuel's eyes on her. When she turned, he quickly looked away.

"Won't you folks stay for lunch?" invited Granny Jewel.

"Land sakes, I guess not," said Mike. We've driven all this way, I guess we need to stick our feet in the ocean. We're staying at the Atlantic Beach Hotel so it's a hop and a skip to the water."

Peggy glanced at Samuel, his overly polite expression a symptom of utter boredom.

"Sarah, will you run over to Mary's and give her Laney's shirt that was left here yesterday. Maybe Samuel would like to go with you."

Like a gazelle, both sprang to their feet. Sarah grabbed the tiny, neatly folded shirt off the hall table, held the door for Samuel, then hurried off the porch.

On the sidewalk, Samuel easily matched Sarah's rapid stride. "I guess we can slow down now. We're out of danger. Tell your mama I'll always be grateful to her for helping us escape."

Sarah laughed. "If I have to hear the story about Spooky's rescue again, I'll scream." She hurried to explain. "Not that I wasn't grateful for your help! I was. If it hadn't been for you, my cat would be lost forever."

"I can thank Spooky for my being here today," admitted Samuel.

"What ever do you mean, Samuel?" asked Sarah, stopping in front of Mary and Morgan Stewart's house.

"Well, my parents kept talking about what happened in the pasture that day, and wondering how you all were getting along, and before we knew it, we were planning a trip to the seashore—and here we are!"

Morgan Stewart came to the door. "I thought I heard voices." He swung the door wide. "Come in and sit awhile. Mary is hanging out a load of wash and I'm sitting on Laney. Hmmm, it seems strange to say 'baby sitting', but if that's what the experts say, I guess that's what I'm doing."

Fearing another session of sitting politely in a living room, making small talk, Sarah protested quickly. "Oh, no, Mr. Stewart. We can't stay. I'm just returning Laney's shirt." She turned to her friend. "I'd like you to meet my neighbor, Morgan Stewart." She turned to Morgan. "This is Samuel Lawrence. He lives on a farm outside Raleigh."

Samuel, the taller of the two, firmly grasped Morgan Stewart's hand, pumping it vigorously. When he finally released the older man's hand, Morgan asked, "How do you two know each other? Do you go to the same school?"

"No, sir," answered Sarah, holding out the shirt, "It's a long story, and we don't have time to stop. Samuel and his parents are here on vacation and they are on their way to the beach." Sarah inched slowly toward the door, Samuel close behind. When they were on the sidewalk, Morgan heard the back door slam.

"Mary, come look."

"What is it, Morgan?" Mary dropped her bag of clothes pins on the chair.

"Tom and Jewel's granddaughter has another love sick fellow in tow. I declare, she collects boys like I used to collect stamps." Mary slipped her arm around her husband's waist and watched the couple walk away. "They grow up so fast. It seems like yesterday she was running around in pig tails."

"The boys better not start coming around here until Laney is at least forty years old."

Mary laughed. "Morgan, there's not a man alive that wants to hand his daughter over to another. But, it happens."

Mike and Janie Lawrence were getting in their car as Sarah and Samuel walked up. He turned quickly to Sarah. "I know it's short notice, but could I come calling tonight? My folks are tired, and they'll probably turn in early, but I'd really like to come over since we'll only be here a short time."

"Sure. We can go to the movies, or, I'll give you a tour of Beaufort." He grabbed her hand and gave it a squeeze.

"Great! I'll see you after supper," he said, flashing a wide grin.

After supper, Sarah took a long bath. *I think I'll wear my white sun-back dress tonight, and pin my hair up. Some red nail polish with matching lipstick should be perfect. Samuel has never seen me fixed up for a date.* She closed her eyes, inhaling the fragrance of her grandmother's lavender soap.

"Sarah, are you going to be in the bathroom all night?" yelled Joshua from the other side of the door.

"I just got in here, pest." She could hear his voice in the upstairs hall.

"Mama, Sarah's been in the bathroom for hours. I gotta go. I gotta go right *now.*" Sarah could hear her mother's soothing voice, but could not understand what she was saying. Soon, she heard her name called.

"Sarah, could you hurry, dear? Your brother is miserable."

"Yes, Mama," she called, sighing audibly. *Someday I'm going to marry a rich man and live in a house that has two bathrooms.*

Sarah opened her closet door and fell across the bed. "Oh, no!" she wailed. "Nancy has my white dress, and she's at camp. I'll have to wear hers! It's not fair!" Sarah, frustrated, buried her face in a pillow.

"Are you all right, honey?" asked Clara from the other side of the door What's all that wailing about?" her voice concerned.

"Come in, Clara," muttered Sarah.

The door opened slowly. "What are you doing stretched out like somebody on their death bed?"

"Oh, Clara, the most *awful* thing has happened! I have a date tonight with the most adorable boy, and Nancy has my favorite dress!"

"Lordy mercy! Here I am thinking something's bad wrong, like an accident, or a heart attack. I never thought it might be something as terrible as not being able to wear your favorite dress on a date." Clara patted Sarah's arm. "Honey, it's not like you don't have another dress.

I see several pretty ones hanging in your closet. This boy's never seen any of them."

"I had my heart set on wearing the white one."

Clara sat in the small chair, covered in pink, flowered material. "Honey, what a person wears don't amount to a hill of beans. It's the person *inside* the clothes that counts." Clara warming to her subject, settled back, making herself more comfortable. "There's plenty of poor, but honorable folks with pure hearts, that wear patched clothes. Lots of people in the history books started out poor, like Mr. Lincoln. Then on the other hand, there's folks what can afford fancy clothes and diamond rings and such." Clara tilted her chin, eyes on the ceiling. Sarah knew she was far from making her point. "They look honorable, but can have a heart as black as midnight." Clara rolled her eyes. "Now you take that high-minded cousin of yours. You could dress her up in clothes fit for the queen of England, and she'd *still* be one aggravating, cruel piece of flesh. Why I . . . ."

From somewhere in the house, they heard Granny Jewel's voice. Clara stood. "It sounds like somebody else needs me. Now don't you forget what I told you. Whatever frock you wear, make sure it's my sweet Sarah on the inside, and what's on the outside won't matter."

"I love you, Clara."

"I know you do, and I love you better than the flowers in May."

By the time Samuel arrived, a light rain was falling. "This will cancel your tour of Beaufort," said Sarah, disappointed. Samuel, unable to take his eyes off of Sarah, merely nodded.

"Anything you want to do is fine with me," he added agreeably. Nancy's crisp, brightly colored dress complemented the girl's tall, graceful figure.

"The Wake of the Red Witch is playing at the theater," said Sarah.

"That sounds fine," Samuel added quickly. "I heard it's real good. I don't get to the picture show very much, cause we live so far out in the country."

Armed with popcorn, candy and Coca-Cola, they enjoyed the movie of drama and adventure. When the movie was over they noticed the rain had stopped. "Let's walk along Front Street, Samuel. We can look in the store windows."

"It will give us a chance to stretch our legs," he added. "I'm not used to being folded up in a chair for two hours."

"I want you to see my grandfather's boat. He takes my brother and me fishing a lot during the summer."

"I've never been fishing."

"It's a lot of fun, Samuel. I can ask Papa Tom to takes us tomorrow morning, if you want to go." Sarah looked troubled. "My little brother is going to want to go."

"That's fine," he said, taking her hand.

The streets were darker when they left the downtown area. Sarah led the way as they walked out on one of the many docks on the waterfront. She pointed at a rowboat gently bobbing in the black water. "That's my grandfather's boat," she said proudly.

"*That* little boat?" Samuel took a step backward, toward land. "You go out in the ocean in *that*?"

"We don't go way out in the ocean, silly. We fish in the inlet." Sarah studied her friend. "Uh, you do know how to swim, don't you?"

"I've been swimming in a farm pond all my life. I don't know if you could call it swimming, or just staying afloat."

"Let's go and talk to my grandfather."

"Tomorrow is your last day, sweetheart," said Papa Tom sadly. "There's nothing I'd like better than to go fishing with you and your brother." Joshua had set up a howl the minute Sarah said the word, 'fishing.'

"None of Sarah's other boyfriends let me go out in the boat with them." An icy stare from his sister discouraged any further comments.

Papa Tom rose from the chair beside his beloved radio. "Samuel," he said, "in order to catch fish, you have to get up mighty early. Do you think you can be here by six o'clock?"

"Gosh, Mr. Mitchell, before six o'clock the cows, pigs, chickens and goats are fed. The tractor is gassed, oil's checked and she's ready to go. 'Bout that time, Mama calls us to breakfast. We mostly eat ham and eggs, grits, toast, stewed apples, fresh milk and home made biscuits. After breakfast, we turn the animals out to pasture, and muck out stalls. By then, it's getting on toward six o'clock, and we head for the fields . . . ."

"I'm sorry I asked," interrupted Papa Tom.

Chapter 17

Sarah, dressed in shorts and old shirt, was up and ready before Mr. Peavy tuned up. Old sneakers, toes out, squeaked with every step as she moved about the kitchen. *These shoes have lost their 'sneak,'* she decided. *Tomorrow when we go to Raleigh, I'll leave them behind in Granny's trash can.* Sarah paused, staring out the back door. *I may be too busy to come back next summer. I may even want to stay in Raleigh with all my friends.* She laid slices of bread on the counter, smeared them with peanut butter and jelly and slapped the slices together. *This may not be a farm breakfast, but these soggy sandwiches will taste mighty good in about two hours, and this lemonade may not taste like Clara's, but at least it's wet.* Animal crackers and apples topped the menu.

Soon, Papa Tom and Joshua appeared at the kitchen door. "Grab a bowl of Rice Krispies and a glass of orange juice." ordered Sarah. Before they could sit down, they heard a light tap on the front door. Sarah hurried to welcome their guest. "Would you like a bowl of cereal, Samuel?" she asked, noting Samuel's bright eyes and eager expression.

"Oh, no thanks. I ate at a diner on the Morehead City waterfront. The waitress wanted to know if I was going deep sea fishing." He gave Sarah a slow smile. "I told her, yep, I was going fishing, but probably not in the deep sea."

"Papa Tom," asked Joshua, between mouthfuls of crispy cereal, "Do you think the motor will work today?" Samuel's smile vanished, replaced with a look of alarm.

"Does the engine break down often?"

"Oh, no," said Papa Tom, winking at Joshua. "It works most of the time."

Joshua interrupted. "If the motor quits on an outgoing tide, we'll be swept out to sea and end up in Portugal."

"Stop your foolishness, Joshua," said Sarah sharply. Turning to Samuel, "They're teasing, Samuel. Don't pay them any attention."

"We always carry oars and oar locks. They never break down," explained the grandfather.

"Do you know how to row a boat, Sarah?" Samuel asked shyly.

"Sarah's been rowing a boat since she was in pigtails. Joshua's pretty good, too. I call them my auxiliary power," explained Papa Tom.

Soon, the little group was hurrying toward the waterfront. The wagon, with the motor inside, bounced with every crack in the sidewalk, the sound interrupting the still, quiet morning.

When they reached the end of the dock, Sarah held the picnic basket, while Samuel helped lift the motor into the boat. When all were seated, Papa Tom pulled the starter cord. The motor sputtered and came alive after the second pull. Papa Tom shoved off from the dock and pointed the bow toward the channel. Skimming across the glassy, smooth water, Samuel twisted and turned, trying to see all of this new and amazing world at one time. A pair of playful dolphin came alongside, so close you could hear them breathe. Joshua, in the bow, swung his thin, brown legs over the side and held out his arms. "I can fly, Samuel," he called over the sound of the motor.

"I'd like to try that, if I wasn't so long legged."

Sarah laughed. "Your feet would drag in the water, and slow us down."

Outer banks ponies, grazing in the marsh, raised their heads, curious that anyone would be on the water this early. Samuel nudged Sarah. "Look!" he exclaimed, "there's a pelican. I know that's what it is, because I saw a picture of one in a book."

When they reached the inlet, the water was now choppy with waves that rocked the small boat. Shafts of gold radiated from the eastern horizon, turning the pink sky to a soft blue. The only sounds were the cry of sea birds diving for minnows, and the gentle lapping of water on the side of the boat.

"God is in this place," Samuel whispered. "I can feel His breath on my face." He turned to Sarah. "I feel closer to Him here, than in church."

"I know, Samuel. I feel the same way."

Lines overboard, Papa Tom slowed the tiny engine. "This is your moment, Samuel. Hold this line, and when you feel a tug, pull it in!"

"Yes sir, Mr. Mitchell." Samuel jammed his straw hat farther down on his head and gripped the line. Joshua fished from the other side, not needing any instruction.

Papa Tom headed the boat along the edge of a submerged shoal. In a few minutes, Samuel yelled, "There's something on the line. It's pulling harder than that stubborn old jackass back home. Glory be! I must have caught a whale!" Joshua and Sarah clapped hands over their mouths trying not to laugh. "It's a great big fish," announced Samuel, pulling in a sleek, silver Spanish mackerel.

"I wish we had a telephone," said Papa Tom. "I'd call Clara and tell her to change the lunch menu from . . ."

Before he could finish, Joshua punctuated the salt sea air with a war whoop. "I got one! I got one! Soon a handsome bluefish was flopping in the bottom of the boat. "Don't get near his mouth," Sarah cautioned. "Bluefish have sharp teeth."

"Now wouldn't that be something if I went home with my finger bandaged? No one would believe it when I told them a fish bit me."

Several more were caught before the tide, which had been coming in, slacked and began to ebb. "That's it for today, kids," announced Papa Tom. "No self-respecting fish is going to bite with the sun high in the sky, and the tide running out."

Sarah passed out sandwiches and cups of cold lemonade from the thermos. *I'll be far from here tomorrow*, she thought. *We should be getting close to home by this time.* A feeling of sadness stole over her. She looked at her grandfather, happily munching on an apple. Their eyes met, and he rewarded her with one of his famous broad winks. Eyes misty, she whispered, "I'm going to miss you, Papa."

"I know, my dear girl, and your granny and I will miss you. But, you have to get back. There's a brand new school year waiting. Your daddy and your other grandparents are counting the minutes till their loved ones are back. All your friends are anxious to tell you about their summer."

Sarah smiled. "You almost make it sound good." Sarah put her hands on her hips, and cocked her head. "You and Granny Jewel will have to move to Raleigh. I suggest that every year, and every year you refuse."

Papa Tom pointed at one of the fish in the bottom of the boat. "See that fish. That's what happens when you take him out of the water. It would be the same with me if I lived away from the coast."

Joshua dove in his grandfather's lap, rocking the tiny boat. "Papa Tom, don't you get all stiff like that fish. We'll just keep coming back every summer."

Sarah looked out across the bar, her eyes resting on Fort Macon. It seemed an eternity since she and Porter had spent a day there.

"OK, crew, we're heading for port. If we hurry, there will be time to clean fish and fry our catch. They'll be the freshest fish you'll ever eat, Samuel."

Clara, anticipating a bucket of fish, had prepared corn bread, slaw, clam fritters and baked beans. Fresh fried fish completed the menu.

After lunch, Sarah and Samuel went out on the front porch. "I have to get back, Sarah. My parents may want the car so they can go sightseeing. We're going back home tomorrow, too." He grinned. "Farmers can't be gone from home for too long. There's too much to do."

"Samuel, I know I promised to write this summer, but I was so busy . . ."

"That's all right. I stayed busy, too. Maybe when the state fair is in town, we could meet at the agricultural building. I'm going to be showing my new calf."

"Oh, that would be fun! We can eat cotton candy and hot dogs, and ride the rides."

"We can hold hands and kiss at the top of the ferris wheel," added Samuel. After a few moments, he rose. "I have to tell your family what a great time I had."

"You've told them several times all ready."

"I could never thank them enough for today. As long as I live, I'll never forget my first boat ride and catching my first fish."

Sarah walked slowly to her bedroom, slid her suitcase from under the bed and opened it. *Why does it seem I just unpacked,* she wondered, emptying dresser drawers. Her mother stuck her head in the door before she finished.

"Don't pack all your dresses. Leave something nice, because Herb and Miriam want us to have dinner with them." She sighed. "It's a farewell meal."

"Mama, do you feel sad about leaving?"

"Oh, yes. I feel like a terrible weight is sitting on my chest. But, I'm excited about seeing your father and all our friends."

"Was it hard to leave home when you and daddy got married?"

"Hmmm, Sarah," she said thoughtfully. "When I fell in love with your father, I would have followed him anywhere on earth. Nothing else mattered as much as being with him."

Sarah had trouble picturing her parents young and in love. "Nancy would think that was very romantic," she said, smiling. Sarah made a mental note to write her friend when she got home.

Miriam and Herb Mitchell had transformed the spacious old house into a gracious home. Wedding gifts, which had been packed away in boxes, now decorated the wide halls and high-ceilinged rooms. The dining room table was complete with white damask cloth, delicate china and silver candelabra. A bouquet of late summer roses graced the center of the table.

Miriam, wearing a white, organdy apron was rushing from the kitchen to the dining room. "Let me help, Aunt Miriam," offered Sarah.

"That would be wonderful. If you would fill the water glasses, I'll finish making a pitcher of iced tea."

A blast of heat greeted Sarah when she went into the kitchen. There were two floor fans that only managed to stir up more hot air. "I hope you all don't mind if we invited Miss Nettie. She has been such good company this summer while I was here all day working on the house."

"Miss Nettie is like family, Aunt Miriam. I catch myself almost calling her 'Aunt Nettie.'"

"She would love that, Sarah. You know, family doesn't have to be someone you are related to. Miss Nettie is tied to our family through heart strings."

"Peggy, dear, I am amazed at how your children have grown this summer," noted Miss Nettie Blackwell, slowly sipping clam chowder from the side of a spoon.

"Yes, Miss Nettie, it must have something to do with the salt sea air. All three are two inches taller and brown as a berry."

Oh brother, thought Sarah. *That's just what I need, two more inches! If I don't stop growing, I'll have to date boys on stilts.*

After the meal, Miriam insisted on leaving the dishes. "I can wash dishes any time. It will be awhile before I see my Raleigh family again. School opens Monday, and we'll be too busy to come and visit." Miriam turned to Sarah. "What are your plans this year? Are you going out for sports, or joining any organizations?"

"I don't know, Aunt Miriam. Uh, I may join the Future Teachers club." She felt guilty when she saw her aunt's reaction. Sarah had never seen her look so happy. *The only reason I'd join is because there are so many people in the club. I wouldn't have to worry about being asked to do anything.*

Daylight faded to darkness. Miss Nettie gave each a hug, and hurried home. After tearful farewells, Papa Tom, his arm around his daughter, Granny Jewel, holding Joshua's hand, and Sarah with Amy in her arms, turned toward home. When they got to the corner, Sarah heard her uncle's voice.

"Sarah, could you wait a minute? I have something I want to ask you."

Sarah paused, "Sure, Uncle Herb."

"Well, you see, uh . . . that is . . . your Aunt Miriam and I want to start a family. Are you planning to come back next summer? We'll need your help if we have a new baby."

"I will, Uncle Herb. I promise I'll be back and spend my seventeenth summer right here in Beaufort."

If you enjoyed Sixteenth Summer . . .

Sarah returns to Beaufort during the summer of her seventeenth year. Expecting to clerk in the family grocery store, Sarah is, instead, given the job of being a companion to her aunt, Miriam Mitchell, who is expecting her first child.

There is a feud at Sarah's grandparent's home. Papa Tom insists the new grandchild will be a boy, but Granny Jewel in her wisdom about such things, knows the baby is a girl.

Miriam's sister from New York arrives a bashful wren, but soon emerges a butterfly when she is taken under the wing of the Mitchell women.

Sarah falls in love with a handsome young crew member aboard The Lovely Lady when she steams into Beaufort. Sarah is no match for the young man's charm and flattery. Ready to follow him to the ends of the earth, Sarah is devastated when he sails away without notice. Is there no antidote for a broken heart? Perhaps the cure is as far away as Ohio.

CPSIA information can be obtained at www.ICGtesting.com
Printed in the USA
BVOW010159131011

273535BV00003B/8/P

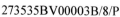

9 781467 034845